Big Brother and Little Brother

By Gary Hinson

For information, or to order additional copies, please contact:

Beacon Publishing Group
P.O. Box 41573 Charleston, S.C. 29423
800.817.8480| beaconpublishinggroup.com

Publisher's catalog available by request.

ISBN-13: 978-1-949472-17-2

ISBN-10: 1-949472-17-2

Published in 2020. New York, NY 10001.

First Edition. Printed in the USA.

Table of Contents

Introduction

A firstborn son entered this world with a glisten in his eyes revealing something special about the child. His parents felt he could do no wrong. He was special because of his ability, appearance, and will.

Years later, another son was born unexpectedly and unwanted. He was growing up alone in a cold world during the depression of the 1930s. The big brother recognized the loneliness of his little brother and he decided he would ensure the young boy was treated fairly in life.

A bond occurred between the two that would change their lives forever.

Chapter One
Johnny is Born

The time was a cold November night in 1923. Nervously, a waiting husband sat on the front porch rolling a smoke on this starry night. He waited for the arrival of his first child in the deep East Texas woods.

A female neighbor, Elizabeth, was assisting his wife, Lillian, in childbirth. He walked under the stars praying to God that his wife and child would come through the duress without trouble.

The chimney top was barely smoking. The thin, blonde-haired man gathered some firewood and went inside to place it inside the fireplace. The old wood house was hard to warm because of no interior walls and it sat on large oak blocks allowing the cold air to penetrate through the old wood floor.

He sat in a chair hearing the pains of childbirth. After several minutes, he heard the cry of a newborn.

The neighbor brought the baby, wrapped in a blanket to the father, William. He held the baby and stared into its sparkling blue eyes. The baby provided a grin to his father.

The neighbor says, "William, what do you think of your baby boy?"

"I think he's the prettiest baby I've ever seen. We're

going to call him Johnny Will Holland."

She replies, "He's sure a pretty thing. I'll take him to Lillian and see if I can help her anymore."

The year passed and the second spring after his birth had Johnny out doing chores with his father. William gave the child small chores, but he completed them quickly and wanted more to do. William is fascinated by the little blonde-haired son's energy and ability to get things done.

One day, William had cut several loads of firewood. Little Johnny wanted to help. So, his father shows him where to stack the cut firewood. William goes to town to buy some liquor and tells the boy to keep stacking. He thinks his son will give up after stacking some of the firewood.

When he returns just before dark, Johnny was stacking the last piece. He can't believe his eyes that the little boy had stacked all the wood that afternoon.

At bedtime, little Johnny watches, from his open window, the stars that sparkle across the sky. He is amazed at how many there are on a clear night. When he tires of watching them, he falls asleep where he lay.

One day, Johnny and his father rode the wagon to town when an old man and his family are in an old pickup driving toward them. He came within inches of hitting them.

The fortyish year man yells to William as he drives by, "Get off the road, you cracker."

Johnny asks, "Why did that man call you cracker?"

"He's mean and doesn't respect people who may not have as much as him. That devil's name is Thomas

Major."

From then on, Johnny would never forget that name.

A few years pass and Lillian was expecting another baby. This time, the baby was a female and she only lived through part of the night.

Johnny saw that his parents were deeply saddened from the loss and that caused him to be sad. They buried the infant in the back of the pasture in a small pine box with a small cross staked in the ground above it. The five-year old Johnny will never forget this day as the rain starts during the time of Elizabeth saying words from the bible. The three of them stand together as the neighbor prays across from them.

As the rain began to pour, the four walked toward the house.

Johnny started school and had listened to the children talking and laughing on the first morning. At that moment, the teacher slammed a paddle against the top of her desk. It was her first day to teach there.

She harshly says, "Be quiet! I don't want to hear another word from any of you unless you raise your hand and I say you can speak. You shall call me Miss Calley at all times."

Johnny doesn't know what to think of such a person. His parents or anybody else never yelled like that at him.

She assigned books to each of the children. When the time came for Johnny to get his book, he looked the middle-age woman over. She gave a quick glimpse at him and continued calling names.

He returned to his desk and realized that she was

probably the ugliest woman he had ever seen. She had a long hook nose and black coarse hair. She had more hair under her arms and on her legs than his father. She was so thin that her veins in her arms pop out. On top of that, she had body odor and long hairs that dangled from her moles on her face and body.

During the day, she swung children in their desks like a bale of hay across the room into corners if they didn't pay attention to what she was saying. By the end of the day, she had put the fear of God in all the children.

Johnny hadn't informed his parents of the crazy teacher. He thought that all teachers might be like that.

Johnny completed the school year without getting swung into a corner. Miss Calley doesn't return the next year as a teacher. Luckily, he has a young teacher that isn't crazy for the next few years.

Occasionally, Johnny saw Thomas Major and even when he doesn't, he saw signs of him. Like whiskey bottles that he and his oldest son threw out in front of his family's little house. He wondered why his father doesn't stand up to them. He only turned his head when they insulted him.

Johnny excelled at everything he did, but his father and mother were dirt poor.

He asked his father while they sat under a shade tree in the pasture resting after working all morning, "Why are we so poor?"

"Well, me and your pretty mother got married when we were sixteen years old. Our parents didn't like us marrying. Her father thought she would be marrying down by marrying me and he was right. We're the black sheep of our families. So, we can't get help from any of them. If I didn't hire myself, doing odd chores out, to the local people, I couldn't pay the mortgage for our little place. We grow and sell our vegetables. You know, I kill most of what we eat. I'm thirty years old and scared to have another child. You're a big help around the place when I'm not around. In fact, you're going to have to fill my roll even more than you do. Like I said, I'm behind on the mortgage payment and I need to go off and earn some real money. I'll send your mother a monthly check to pay for the mortgage and anything else that yawl need. I know you're only eight years old, but I believe you and your mother can take care of everything while I'm gone. Can you do it?"

"I will do my best."

"I know you will."

His father had found a job cutting timber in the region. He will live in a logging camp wherever he cuts timber until he earns enough to pay the mortgage off.

Johnny and his voluptuous mother worked together well. While he was in school, she drives the wagon to town for supplies about every two weeks.

A few months have passed since his father departed. His mother was usually home when he arrives from school, but she isn't there.

Johnny went on about his chores but worrying of his mother's absence. She finally arrived about dark. Johnny doesn't ask why she's late and she doesn't tell him anything.

As the months pass by, she continued to come in late. He never questioned her, and the brown hair mother never volunteered any information.

Johnny had become popular with the teacher and

students. Even the few neighbors, on his way home, waved at him when he rode by on his horse bareback.

He and his mother worked every afternoon and Saturdays until dark. They rested on Sundays by reading to one another and taking a nap together. She read the letters to him that William wrote to them.

After seven months, William returned home and soon after arguing began between him and Lillian. Johnny had hardly ever heard his mother and father have a cross word. His mother cried a lot. The house was like a graveyard, but Johnny was still treated well by each of them.

William takes Johnny almost everywhere he goes, but sometimes he is gone when he returns from school and he doesn't return until the next day. Things are different now and Johnny knew it. It will be something that he will have to live with.

One day, Thomas Major was at the feed store when William and Johnny were there.

Major sees William loading up his wagon and says, "If you're in my way out there on that road, I'll run you off the road, cracker."

Johnny watched for his father's reaction and there was none. Major had his three sons with him and the oldest son, Quincy at eighteen years old, smiled as his father belittled William. Johnny wanted his father to say or do something, but he doesn't.

Johnny is hesitant to say something to his father on the way home, but he did.

"Daddy, why do you let that man treat you that way?"

"Son, as long as he doesn't put his hands on me, I'm not going to fight a loudmouth like that."

"I will when I get big."

The ride was quiet the remainder of the way home.

Johnny turned nine years old and his mother baked him a cake. He wished and blown all nine candles out. They gave him a single shot sixteen-gauge shotgun for his birthday present. This enabled him to help kill game animals for the family.

He and his father hunted the river bottom of the Neches River. They killed feral hogs, squirrels, rabbits, raccoons, and an occasional deer.

One hunt in the afternoon after school, Johnny got lost in the bottom. His father attempted to draw him closer by shooting his gun. Johnny cannot seem to get closer despite his repeated attempts. Finally, the shots stop, and he walked through briars and brush after walking miles before he came upon a dirt road. He stopped at the first and only house on the road. It's a black homesteader living out in the middle of nowhere. The black man brought him in his wagon to the end of the road after midnight and Johnny walked the rest of the way home arrived just before daylight.

His mother cooked him breakfast as he cleaned the squirrels he killed. After he finished, he cleaned up and went to school. He took getting lost in stride. He didn't complain about anything.

The young girls at school are attracted to Johnny. He smiled to them but didn't know what to say to them. They initiated conversation and he responds with simple answers. They liked him despite his lack of conversing.

A new teacher had started this year and she noticed the girls and boys all like Johnny. She didn't like it and complained about it in class to the twenty-nine students. Even Major's younger sons didn't hate Johnny, but they like the teacher complaining that Johnny can do nothing wrong according to the class. The Major brothers just found what they needed in the fixated teacher —confidence.

When the boys tell their father of the teacher's resentment toward the Holland boy, he says, "The little cracker will end up following in his cracker daddy's footsteps. If he gets uppity, the teacher will put him down and if she doesn't do enough, you three put him in his place."

The boys at the one room schoolhouse pick on an eight-year old girl who is plain and poor. Johnny is usually mostly quiet. The teacher usually doesn't say anything about the abuse to the young girl, but when Johnny calls her a sardine, the teacher goes crazy slapping him all over the face for nearly a half-minute. He doesn't move and doesn't cry as she viciously hit him with obvious hatred for the boy.

Johnny went home and never mentioned the smacking he took. He was saddened the next few days and realized he never called anybody a name and never would again. The teacher seemed to warm up to him in his lowest humility, but he would never forget her intentional humiliation of him.

The school year went by and Johnny knew that life will not be kind as he thought no matter what he accomplishes.

Chapter Two
Joey is Born

During the summer, Johnny discovered he had a baby brother. There wasn't any fanfare with the newborn Joey. The baby was born healthy and joyful, but there is gloom hanging over the Holland house. The parents continued the repression of conversation and closeness.

Johnny started a new school year with a new teacher, Mrs. Gray, and that is a relief for Johnny. His popularity continues to rise, and the teacher treats each student the same. She is a middle-age married woman with an ordinary appearance. He thought she looked somewhat mean, but she never raises her voice at anyone. Although she does speak with firmness.

The Major boys walked home in the opposite direction that Johnny does and so far, that has worked in his favor. Unfortunately, the three boys followed him out of school one afternoon. The oldest Major boy named Clayton Ray, C.R., was sixteen years old, behind him was Jock at fourteen years old, and the youngest, Willard, was twelve years old.

The nine-year old, Johnny, was scared and ran as fast as he could. As they ran after him, he found a kick he didn't know he had. They decided the effort wasn't worth it and gave up the chase.

As the year went on, C.R. quit school and the two younger brothers were left to deal with Johnny. One afternoon, Johnny stayed after school to get extra lessons from the teacher in math. When he headed home, the two Major boys waited for him about a hundred yards from the school with his horse.

He doesn't see them until they step out from the brush thirty feet in front of him. He came to a halt. Contemplating what he should do, he walked slowly toward them. When he attempted to walk around them, they stood in his way. He began to force himself through them, but they grabbed him. He struggled with them until Jock punched him in the stomach. The larger boys have the edge on him, and he can't do anything about it. Once they beat him to the ground, he stays down aching in pain.

Jock says, "This is to let you know that if you get to big for your britches, we will beat your butt again."

Johnny stayed quiet as he lay on the dirt road holding his stomach.

He tells his mother and father about the beating he took from the Major boys. His father tells him, "Tell the teacher what they did."

Johnny is ashamed and doesn't tell the teacher anything.

The school year ended, and Johnny returned to working all day during the summer in the gardens his father planted in the spring. He maintained and harvests the garden daily except Sundays. His father worked for other people has much as possible. On Sundays, Johnny and his father went fishing in the morning and rested in the afternoon. His mother fried the fish, they caught, that evening.

Joey played on the porch and in the dirt most of the day. Johnny doesn't give him much attention and neither do his parents. He saw his mother occasionally feed the child. Most of the time, she's busy canning vegetables.

The new school year began, after Labor Day, with a few new 1st graders, but the remainder of the class remained the same including Jock and Willard. Jock had grown about two inches over the summer, but so did Johnny. Willard looked the same as he did before the summer.

Mrs. Gray allowed the children to play softball at breaktime in the afternoon. Johnny caught on quick and gradually became first baseman for his team in the spring.

Mrs. Gray thought the children played well and suggested to the Superintendent that a game should be played against another area school.

He made it happen and a game materialized in a pasture between the two schools that was separated by sixteen rural miles. Johnny was the starting first baseman for the school. He played a flawless game except he missed a catch but was still able to recover and get the runner out. His team won 4-0 with him getting two runs. Some of the boys raised him up and carried him on their shoulders to the bus. He is the captain of the team.

Whether the girls played or not, all they talked about was Johnny. It was like Johnny had a spell on him that he could do no wrong. The last day of school was the next day and Mrs. Gray let the children play games since they all passed to the next grade.

Johnny was back tending to the garden for another summer while his father worked for other farms in the area.

One day while resting in the shade, Johnny watched dirty little Joey play in the dirt. Johnny had never seen his father acknowledge the boy and the mother does the minimum for the child to survive. He thought about the girl that the boys made fun of and no one has anything to do with her. She seems kind of dumb in school and he sees his little brother with probably the same fate. He knows how the Major boys had been mean to him.

He walked over to the little boy and asked him what he's doing, and the child can't answer except for some babble. The child wasn't being taught to talk. He attempted to teach the child some words that he may understand if told enough.

As the summer days continued, Johnny was teaching his little brother to talk and understand things more. Little Joey liked his older brother and he followed him wherever he went. In late afternoon, Johnny washed the dirt off himself and Joey at the water pump.

The father noticed Johnny helping Joey more and more. He said, "Johnny, don't waste too much of your time on that kid."

He replied, "If I don't, who will?"

He nor the mother said anything.

Occasionally after supper, Johnny takes Joey out to lie in the yard and watch the stars. Johnny told him what little he knew about the cosmos. Despite Joey's handicap for speaking, he learned quickly with Johnny teaching him.

Another summer winds down and Johnny returned to school. Nothing has changed except a few more first graders. Jock and Willard are back, and they haven't grown any taller while Johnny has grown another couple of inches. Mrs. Gray always separates the two brothers as she does all the siblings in class.

Johnny doesn't hang with any group of children. He was friendly to all the class except the Major brothers and kept his distance from two other boys that talked with the two brothers. They're all older than him. He saw them all staring at him quite often. They scared him, but not as much as they thought.

When Johnny got home in the afternoons after his six-mile bareback ride from school, Joey was there to meet him. He immediately took the little fella under his wings as he does the chores at the farm.

Johnny says, "You know, I should call you 'dirt boy' since you're always dirty."

Little Joey laughs.

Johnny turned twelve and his mother and father always get him a gift on his birthday. He received a saddle for his horse. He wondered why he needed it and his father must show him how to put it on the mare, Gypsy. Once he rode on it, he realized how much more comfortable the riding became.

Once he rode to school on the saddled horse, everyone there told him how nice the saddle was except the Major boys and their two friends. He allowed the horse to roam free around the schoolhouse while he was in class. When he got through with class in the afternoon, he whistled, and Gypsy came running.

One early spring afternoon, Johnny went to fetch a foul ball where Willard and his two friends stood.

Johnny bent over to pick it up and Willard pushed Johnny and he retaliated with a right cross to the fifteen-year old Willard's chin. Down goes Willard and on top was Johnny pinning him down to the ground. Suddenly, seventeen-year old Jock grabbed him off Willard and slings him across the dirt. Quickly, Johnny regains his balance and both brothers come after him. He sees Gypsy by the school and runs for it and rides away from the two.

Summer arrived and his little brother turned three without anyone remembering or caring to know about it. Johnny knew it was in the summer but when he doesn't remember. He had taught Joey how to do many of the chores and the father took notice. He was the little boy doing chores during the day and not completing them to the father's satisfaction.

When Johnny arrived from school, he heard Joey crying and his father yelling, "Your brother could do anything I told him to do when he was your age. Get out of my sight before I whip your ass.

Johnny asks little Joey, "Was your chore stacking firewood?" He nods his head.

"C'mon and I'll help you."

They stacked all the firewood and they watched the stars appear in the sky that early evening. "Where's the north star?"

Joey points at it and smiles. "That's right. What kind of moon do we have tonight?"

Joey replies, "Half."

They smiled at each other as Johnny nods his head. Their mother called them for supper.

Jock didn't return to school this school year and Willard was alone at school. He stared at Johnny a lot. He paid Willard no mind. One day in class, Johnny felt something hit his ear. He turned to find Willard had thrown a spitball. He turned back around and doesn't say anything.

When class ended for the day, Johnny followed Willard. Now, Johnny was the same height as him. He grabbed him by the shoulder from behind and yanked him to the ground.

"If you throw a spitball or try anything else to pester me, I'll beat your tail off. Do you hear me?"

Willard nodded his head. Johnny walked away but looked back occasionally because he doesn't trust Willard or any of the Majors.

With Willard no longer a threat, Johnny felt relieved, but it's short-lived as Johnny rode home and the six-feet-one-inch Jock was waiting for him with the family truck blocking the road. He's leaned against the hood of the truck when Johnny rode up on his horse.

The eighteen-year old Jock stepped in the middle of the road and said, "Get off that horse or I'll pull you off."

The thirteen-year old Johnny looked the situation over before he dismounted. He stood with his fists up and Jock went in swinging wildly at the smaller opponent at five-feet-seven-inches. He went under Jock's swings and trips the taller foe to the ground. Once down on the ground, he plummeted the larger opponent until his adversary clinched him around the head. There they are stuck on the ground in each other's grasp. They stay locked up for five minutes until both began to hit each other again. Johnny has given his all and the older and larger enemy still seemed strong.

The wiry Jock said, "Okay, no one wins today. If you rough up Willard again, I'll beat your ass next time or C.R. will do it for me."

The brown-haired Jock drove the truck home and Johnny went home with only a bump under the jaw.

When Johnny arrived home, he doesn't see Joey waiting for him. Johnny asked his father, "Where is Joey?"

"The last time I saw him, he was at the corn patch."

He goes out to look for Joey and found him sitting behind the barn. He looked down at him and saw belt whelps on his back and arms. The little boy wore coveralls with no shirt and no shoes.

"Did Daddy do this to you?"

Joey nodded and cried.

"Why did he whip you?"

"I, I broke jars."

"I'll talk to him about this. I don't like him whipping you this way. Do you want to help me dig some potatoes?"

He nodded.

After they dig the potatoes and wash off, Johnny went to his father. "Daddy, why did you whip Joey like you did?"

"He broke some food jars. That costs me nearly two dollars."

"How did he break more than one jar?"

"By dropping the grocery bag with jars in it."

"Why would they put jars in one bag and that's too heavy for him to carry anyway."

"He grabbed the bag and dropped it without me

seeing him."

"He was trying to help. If he breaks anything else, you take it out of those dollars you give every so often — not on his bare hide."

The father walked away from him. The evening was quiet at the dinner table is as it usually was but not a word was said tonight.

Johnny attempted to ease Joey's mind by climbing out the open window with him and watch the cosmos.

The next afternoon, Johnny arrived home from school and found Joey behind the barn, again.

"He looked over Joey and saw that he hasn't received anymore whelps. He asked, "Why are you behind the barn?"

"Daddy n Momma don't want me by them."

"Did they say that?"

"No. I know."

Johnny knew Joey was right. "I can't help the way they are, but I can be here whenever you need me." He shook his head — knowing Johnny is at school most of the day.

"You holler for me; Joey and I'll try my best to be here."

Joey can only hold his head down. He doesn't have the words to reply and it probably wouldn't matter.

Chapter 3
Major Problems

Willard graduated and Johnny had no more problems with the Major boys at school.

He informed his father of the good news.

The father asked, "Did they give you much trouble at school?"

"They did until a year ago."

"How did you put up with them all those years?"

"By avoiding them, running from them, getting beat-up by them, and fighting them."

"I'm sorry you had to put with all of that. I wished you would've told me. I may've could done something about it."

Johnny shook his head and went about his chores. He doesn't believe his father would have done much except make it worse.

He said to Joey while in the garden, "You'll be starting school after the summer. You can ride Gypsy with me back and forth to school. Before long, you'll be reading and writing. Joey won't be stuck on this farm all day. Are you glad about that?"

"Yep. I can be with you all the time."

"Now, in class, you're going to have to be quiet and do what Mrs. Gray tells you to do. She's a good teacher and I know because I had some bad teachers before she came along."

"I hope she'll like me."

"She treats all the students the same. She isn't mean at all, but she doesn't smile much. So, don't think she dislikes you. Okay?"

"Okay."

On Labor Day weekend, Lillian cut the boys' hair before school started. She cut Joey's brown hair first. It's a quick haircut. When Johnny was getting his haircut, she stroked her fingers through his long blonde hair and told him his hair was beautiful and what a handsome young man he had become.

Joey watched from a distance and knew she never shown him or told him anything that nice. It still hurt him even though he already feels unloved.

While riding to school, Joey asked Johnny, "Why do Momma and Daddy hate me?"

"They don't hate you. I'll have to think about them before I can tell you more."

"You know they hate me. Why do you lie to me?"

"There are things I just don't understand enough to tell you the right answer."

"They hate me. I hope Mrs. Gray don't hate me."

"I already told you, she won't."

All the girls in class have a crush on Johnny. In fact, one of the young boys talked to the girls at lunch and he came up to Johnny.

"Johnny, all the girls want to go with you. They want to know which one you'll go with."

Johnny replied, "Let me sleep on it and I'll tell you

tomorrow."

The first day of school goes well for Johnny and Joey. Johnny asks Joey on the way home, "Did you like school?"

"I liked it."

"Well, what did you like about it?"

"I like Mrs. Gray and I know you're there with me."

"I'm glad you like it. Learn everything you can."

That night, Johnny laid in bed and thought about the girls in class. There were some cute ones that he thought were too young. He thought about the girls his age and had a difficult time deciding between three. One was a dark-haired, blue-eyed girl, but she had a witch face that means she'll be ugly when she got older. Another was a blonde with blue eyes, but she was the jealous type. The last was Elizabeth, a black-haired beauty, with an Indian look about her that Johnny finds sexy.

The next day, Johnny informed the young student that he preferred, Lizzy. The connection was made, and they had lunch together every day. There wasn't much talk, but there's enough to continue meeting.

Johnny and Joey rode to the country store for a hot summer day treat. While at the store, three teenage sisters are outside drinking soda waters. They smiled at Johnny when he walked in the store and now, they waited for him to come out. Joey was drinking his soda water by Gypsy when Johnny came out of the store and is stopped by the girls.

The oldest sister, Loretta, says, "Hello Johnny."

"Hello Loretta, Loraine, and Louise."

"We're going swimming at the creek. Why don't you come with us?"

"Where is your swimming suits?"

"We don't need any and neither do you."

Johnny looked at the girls and they've all smiled at him with a glisten in their eyes. He looked at the three full grown girls and they're not bad looking. The brown-haired Loraine had already graduated; The blonde-haired Loraine had just graduated; The black-haired Louise was a year older than Johnny and still in school.

He said, "I'd like to go, but I have my little brother with me."

Loretta responded, "I think you're scared of us."

"I'll go with yawl. Let me talk to my brother first."

Johnny walked over to Joey. He bent down on one knee to talk with him.

"Joey, I want you to ride Gypsy on home. I'll be home in a little while."

"Why can't I go with you?"

"Well, I got somethings I need to do myself. You get on back home and I'll see you later."

He gave Joey a boost upon Gypsy and patted him on his way.

Johnny turned and walked with the girls to the creek. Joey was curious and turned Gypsy around to find out what Johnny doesn't want him to see. He followed the winding road down to the creek and stopped when he can see it through the trees. He watched as they strip down without any clothes. The girls gathered around Johnny, in the creek, as Joey watched for a few minutes before departing for home.

Johnny doesn't return home until after dark and

immediately went straight to bed.

The next morning, he's slow in getting out of bed.

Joey asked him, "Are you going to do chores this morning?"

"I'll be out there later. You can go ahead and start without me. You know what to do. Dad is off working today. He won't be here to mess with you without me being around you.

Joey ate breakfast and went to milk the cow and gathered the chicken eggs. He walked back to the house for another biscuit and when he neared the house, he heard his mother talk to Johnny.

"Without you here, I would leave this place. I can't leave because you are the only person I love in this whole world."

Johnny responded, "I wish you wouldn't talk that way when Dad and Joey love you."

"I can't help the way I feel."

"Don't worry. I'm not going anywhere for quite a while."

Joey had heard enough and walked to the field to pick beans and peas. It hurt, but he has grown accustomed to it. He contemplated why everyone, including himself, loved Johnny so much. At this stage of his life, he just accepted it without questioning it.

The last year of Johnny's schooling started. He was seventeen years old and Joey was eight. Johnny won't stay with one girl and most of the girls liked it that way. He was available to them all. He won't forget about Joey even with his popularity.

Joey won't stay far from Johnny at school or at

home, he was with him all the time.

Word had been spread about Johnny throughout the area. The Majors don't like a cracker's son gaining popularity.

Thomas said to his boys while sitting on the porch, "Jock and Willard didn't put that boy in his place. C. R., it's your time to put that cracker boy down. If you don't do it, I'll get Quincy and he'll damn sure get it done. As for as that cracker father, I'll take care of him the next time I see him."

So, C.R. and his father waited for Johnny as he and Joey rode to school in the morning. At six feet, 180 pounds, Johnny saw trouble with old man Thomas and C.R. parked in the road. They stood in the middle of the road and waited for Johnny to make the next move. Johnny thought about attempting to ride through them, but he worried about Joey.

He told Joey to ride on to school as he dismounted from Gypsy. Joey is divided whether to wait for his endangered brother or to follow his order. Johnny pats Gypsy on his way with Joey.

C.R. at six-feet one inch and 200 pounds walked to Johnny and started swinging. Johnny backed away from the onslaught and waited for the opportunity to strike his opponent.

Old man Major yelled, "Watch that sly cracker, he's trying to set you up."

Johnny continued, in an attempt, to lure his foe into a mistake, but C.R. cut Johnny off from evading his pursuit. Johnny slammed his right fist hard into C.R.'s nose. Blood came streaming out of his nose, but that doesn't slow him from swinging his fists on Johnny's head. Johnny backed away from the barrage and charged ahead again with both fists hitting his target again and again.

Johnny came out of the slugfest with a bleeding nose, but he landed the more effective blows.

Old man Major yelled to C.R., "Don't stop now, you got him bleeding."

Blood was all over both opponents. Johnny's white tee shirt was redder than white. They stalked about each other jabbing at one another. This was when the fitter Johnny showed his stamina while C.R.'s whiskey drinking, and smoking was getting the better of him.

Old man Major yelled, "Don't slow down now, C.R. You're a grown man. Beat that cracker boy's ass!"

C.R. charged in on Johnny and down went C.R. Johnny walked on to school as his foe was on his hands and knees.

Old man Major said to Johnny as he walks away, "Don't think this is over cracker. If I see you before Quincy does, I'll kick your cracker ass."

Johnny heard his words, but he showed his worth today by beating the second meanest Major boy. He wasn't scared of old man Major or six-feet-six-inch son Quincy.

Joey asked, "Did you win?"

"Yeah. I won."

"They won't bother you anymore. Will they?"

"I don't think we'll ever be rid of the Majors."

When they arrived home, their Mother sees the bloody tee shirt. "Did you get in a fight?"

"Yeah, with the Majors."

"Why are those people so mean?"

"Dad told me the truth several years ago about old man Major. He said they felt they were better than us and they intended to keep it that way."

"Why? Just because they've got a big house and an automobile? They ain't nothin special."

"I believe that makes them think they're better than us. They've sure given me a hard time"

"Oh son, why haven't you told us?"

"I told Dad I thought it was over. I was wrong. It'll never be over with them."

Joey listened to every word and he won't forget it.

Johnny graduated and was approached at the country store by a strange thin man. "Hello, Johnny."

Johnny looked at the mid-thirties stranger and asked. "Hello. How do you know who I am?"

"I've heard about your fighting abilities."

"What do you mean?"

"The word is you've beaten the Major boys and they're the toughest in the county. I make fights happen for money."

"Are you trying to tell me that you want me to fight for money? What is your name?"

"My name is Mr. Rizer and you'll be fighting for money. I get a percentage of the fight purse while the winner gets the larger portion of the purse. The more people that bets on the fight the more money is in the purse. You can bet on yourself if you want."

"Who will I be fighting?"

"The meanest, roughest, toughest sonofabitch I can dig up. How about you and Quincy Major for the first match?"

"If I win, how much money will I make?"

"Anywhere between $100 and $1000. It depends on the draw."

"That's a lot of money."

"All you gotta do is sign a piece of paper agreeing with the terms and we'll be set."

"Where is this piece of paper?"

"I'll draw it up right now if you're willing to fight Quincy Major."

"The fight is going to happen whether I get paid or not. So, I might as well get paid for it."

"You're already learning the fight game. Let's sit down on this porch and we'll get this started."

Chapter Four
The Fight

Johnny worked at the farm as Joey rode Gypsy back and forth to school every day. While Johnny worked, he thought about the upcoming fight with the huge Quincy. He realized Quincy will have the reach on him and a huge weight advantage. No one in the county would dare fight Quincy. Johnny knew that it would take a superhuman effort to beat the massive Quincy.

He knew he will have to put on bulk to absorb the punches and dish out more with strength. The streamlined Johnny began eating six eggs for breakfast instead of three. He bought a body building book for the exercises to bulk up. He believed he already had the stamina and concentrated on his power by using his fists against the stacked hay bales.

Every day, he worked on bulking his body before doing his chores. His father wanted him to come work with him for a while, but he declined because of the upcoming fight.

His father asked him, "Why don't you wanna work for some money. I'll cut you in on the pay."

"I'm getting ready to make some big money."

"Doing what?"

"Fighting Quincy Major."

"You'll be committing suicide against him. The man

is a giant. Who's going to pay you money to get your brains beat in?"

"I have to win to get the money. A fight manager is taking bets throughout the county."

"I thought you was smarter than this. That fella is gonna end up takin off with the money even if you get lucky and win. I think the whole thing is a setup."

"Sometimes, you got to take a chance even if the odds are against you. The fight is going to happen whether I get paid or not."

"That Major has forearms like anvils. Johnny, you've done right your whole life. Now, you're making a big mistake. He's going to leave you addle-brained if he doesn't kill you."

"I've had to fight his three younger brothers and I didn't want to fight them and I'm still here with a sound mind."

"Those other Major boys are about your size. Don't even try to compare them to him. I'm going to bring a gun if he starts killing you."

"It would be best if you don't come at all."

"What kind of father would I be to let you go there by yourself in a mess of rattlesnakes?"

Johnny worried more about his father coming to the fight than he is about himself.

After another week, Mr. Rizer drove up at Johnny's place. "How are you Johnny?"

"I'm doing good. What have you got to tell me?"

"I'm trying to finalize the fight date and time. How about this Saturday at eight o'clock in the evening?"

"It's dark at that time. How are we supposed to fight in the dark?"

"There'll be plenty of lighting there. The place is the crossroad before you get to Willow Creek. I'll pick you up at seven o'clock if that's alright with you."

"Yeah. My father wants to go with me."

"Well, I suppose that will be okay. By the way, the purse is going to be several hundred dollars for the winner."

"Several hundred dollars from this poor ass county?"

"You two are well known around these parts and gambling is in most people's blood. They have money tucked away in their mattresses for the right occasion. I hate to tell you this, but you're a four to one underdog."

Johnny smiled and nodded his head as Rizer walked to his car.

It was the day of the fight and Johnny felt confident after all his training. Joey was out at the barn with Johnny.

Joey said, "I heard at school you were going to fight Quincy Major for a million dollars.

Johnny laughed. "Who told you it was for a million dollars?"

"That's what they're all saying at school."

"That's nonsense. I'm going for a short run. I'll be back in a short while."

Johnny crossed the pasture and jumped the fence before going for his run. The run made his body sweat and that made him feel good as he ran to the front of the house.

His mother came to talk to him. "Your father tells me that you're goin to fight that big ole Major boy or man. Don't you realize that you're just becoming a young man and he has everything in his favor. Use your wits and don't let him get you on the ground. He's too big to get off you. You've always done things that we didn't think possible, but you have always proven us wrong. Prove everybody wrong, again."

"You know, I'll do my best."

Johnny took a nap that afternoon and got up feeling good. He ate some chicken, peas, and cornbread for supper.

A couple hours later, Mr. Rizer drove up. Johnny and his father walked out to the car. Joey walked up and Johnny looked at his father.

Johnny's father said, "He wants to come, and he needs to learn what not to do."

Johnny shakes his head in disapproval.

As they traveled the eight miles on the dirt roads, Johnny realized he must respect his adversary as if he were a wild animal—vicious, dangerous, mad, and non-compassionate, but stay in control and contain the beast.

They arrived and there are plenty of people with their automobiles, wagons, and horses. More continued to pour in at the crossroads before the eight o'clock fight. The temperature was warm for a late October night.

Johnny took his shirt off displaying his muscular 190-pound body while he watched the giant Quincy stare at him from across the road.

Old man Major yelled to William Holland, "The young cracker brought along the old cracker. I'll take care of him as soon as Quincy takes care of junior."

The crowd of over sixty began to holler for the fight to get started and so Mr. Rizer decided to provide the introduction of the fight after confirming the fighters are ready.

He gets on top of the hood of his 1938 Ford Coup automobile and says, "Listen up people!" He holds his hands above his head. "I need a few of you to move your vehicles out of the crossroad. Everybody needs to do that if we're going to get this fight started."

Once the autos are moved, he introduced the fighters. "Listen up people! You all know why you're here tonight. While the kids are Halloweening, we have us a heavyweight bout to watch. On the other side of the road is Quincy Major. The biggest, meanest man in the county at 255 pounds, all six foot six inches of him." Plenty of his supporters are heard at the introduction.

"This side of the road is the blonde wonder, Johnny Holland. At six-foot-tall and 190 pounds, he is quick as a cobra and just as deadly."

He jumped down from his vehicle and got between the two opponents. Joey climbed on top of Rizer's vehicle. "

Rizer says, "The only rules is there will be no gonad kicking and stomping opponent when he is down. You will get one warning and the second will bring about forfeiture of the purse by the disqualified to his opponent. The fight will stop when one fighter waves his arm to quit."

Quincy asked his father, "What did he say?"

"He said to beat the hell of each other. Now, go beat the hell out of that cracker boy."

Rizer waved his hands for them to go at it.

Johnny saw Quincy as an intimidating figure, but he must win for the money and mostly to conquer all the Majors. He has confidence in himself, but he needed to prove it to himself and everybody else.

Johnny evaded Quincy's aggressive attacks, but the crowd wanted action—not just quick moves to avoid punches. He felt the overwhelming power of his larger opponent and realized he couldn't match up blow by blow. He felt he has the power to hurt big Quincy. It was just a matter of when the opportunity arises. Quincy has shown more stamina than Johnny thought he would. Despite the crowd wanting action, he must be patient when to attack. When Johnny saw Quincy's arms going down, he launched an assault on the massive foe. He almost knocked Quincy down.

The whole time the fight continued, old man Major and his sons shouted for Quincy to stomp Johnny in the ground. The crowd had a taste of the action and they craved more. Joey yelled to the top of his lungs for Johnny to beat his foe. Johnny's father watched in amazement as his son seemed to always beat the odds.

Johnny was on the defensive as Quincy unleashed an attack that would take any man out. Johnny sensed futility in winning the fight. He lashed out with all the energy he can muster, but he felt the inevitable coming. He hit Quincy hard enough that got him angry as hell.

Suddenly, Sheriff Gentry and a deputy drove up and started blowing their whistles. They came busting through the crowd, with their heavy-duty flashlights, attempted to stop the fight.

The sheriff shouted out as Johnny tried to keep his distance from the mad Quincy, "Break it up or you're all going to jail! Let's get these two away from each other before someone really gets hurt."

Several men grab hold of Quincy while Sheriff Gentry and his deputy pulled Johnny out of the fracas. Most everyone is hollering for Quincy to be called the winner, but Rizer wasn't saying anything right now.

Sheriff Gentry asked Johnny, "Are you trying to get yourself killed fighting that monster of a man?"

"No. It was a fight I had to fight."

"Well, you're lucky you only got a bloody mouth."

Johnny feels like his ribs have been beaten to pulp.

The six-feet tall Thomas Major makes his way to Rizer wanting his money. Rizer responded, "Not tonight."

Sheriff Gentry said to them, "I said break it up or I'll put your asses in jail including you, Thomas Major."

He responded, "We'll see about this at election time."

"Keep talking and you'll be spending the night in jail."

Sheriff Gentry asked, "Have you cooled down, Quincy?"

"I'll quit if he'll quit."

"You'll quit—won't you boy?"

"Yeah. I'll quit."

Sheriff Gentry told, "Thomas, take Quincy home now or I'll lock you both up."

All the Majors load up in the truck and drive off, but not before, Thomas yells, "Sheriff, I'll see you back working that plow after the election and cracker, I'll be seein yawl soon enough."

The sheriff turns to Johnny, "Have you got a ride?"

He pointed toward Rizer and his vehicle.

The sheriff looked at Rizer and his vehicle. "Where did you come from, stranger?"

"Up north."

"What are you doing around here? Starting up trouble?"

"No, Sheriff. I come to convert some souls."

"Yeah. I bet you've converted some. I just hate to see which way you converted them. If I see you around anymore trouble, I'll bring you in to find out who you really are. Now, get all of you!"

Rizer gets all three of them loaded up and talked with them on the way to the Holland place. "Johnny, you did good against that slab of dumbass. We'll need to talk about your next fight after I let your family out."

William said, "What in the hell are you talking about? Another fight—after that big galoot almost killed my son."

Rizer responds, "Mr. Holland, your son is young. He has a bright future ahead of him."

"Not if you keep lining up fights with the likes of Quincy Thomas."

"You let me take care of that. I've decided to split the purse between the two combatants—$400 dollars apiece. How does that sound?"

"Where's the money?"

"As soon as we stop at your place."

Rizer stopped in front of the Holland home. Joey watched Johnny press his handkerchief against his mouth.

"Are you going to be alright?" Joey asked.

"I think I'll make it."

Rizer pulled the money out and counted the four hundred dollars to Johnny. "How's that for a half-hour of fighting?"

Johnny replied, "Since I survived the fight, I'll have to say that it was worth it, but I had my doubts during the fight."

He handed his father $100. His father asked, "What's this for?"

"It's to help better you and the family. Buy yourself, Joey, and Momma some new clothes."

"Thank you, Johnny."

"I'll see you and Joey inside when I get through talking with Mr. Rizer."

They said their goodnights and Johnny looked at Rizer concerning future fights."

"Johnny, the reason I wanted to talk to you may take a little more time than you are expecting. You are a magnificent specimen of the white race and I've come down here to East Texas after hearing from one of our informants of your potential. Yes, tonight, you were pitted against another older white man, but he is white trash and that's all he'll ever be. We have plans for your future to be a model for our cause."

"What cause?"

"The supremacy of the Aryan Race. We have researched your family and found no traces of inferior races."

"Until you gave me this money, we have been dirt poor. How can we be of a superior bloodline?"

"Despite your lack of family wealth, you fit the physical characteristics of our superman. In a society full of conmen and mixed races, you have slipped through the cracks of superiority. In our world, you'll be a man of deserving entitlement — no longer a footstep for others to use you as if you have no consequence."

"I'm not sure I follow you. How can I get from a nobody to someone of importance?"

"Leave that up to me."

"Whatever you say, Mr. Rizer."

"That's all for tonight. I'll be talking to you in about week. Rest up and goodnight."

Johnny walked into the house and complained of his ribs hurting when he lay down. His mother covered his torso with a tight dressing. He ached all night and for the next week, he rarely got out of his bed.

Joey worried about him and his father realized the beating he taken had consequences. His mother removed the bandages every few days and finds a couple of knots on his ribs.

"You have two broken ribs, Johnny."

Johnny responded, "I feel like they're all broken."

Mr. Rizer came by and Johnny walked out to talk to him without his shirt, but with his bandages on.

"How are you, Johnny?"

"I'm doing a little better than I was when I last saw you."

"Good. I'm trying to get you a fight with a nigger in the county about five miles from here."

"I ain't never fought any of them. What should I expect?"

"I'm sure this one is tough and that means you are going to have to put him down by any means you can—break every bone you can and avoid hitting him in the skull if you can because they have a one-eighth-inch thicker skull than you do. Break his face and hit him with body shots. You were head hunting against

Quincy Major. I don't know how well he can fight but do as I say, and I believe you'll win."

"When are you wanting this fight to happen and how big is this man?"

"The man is six-foot-two inches and 210 pounds—black as an ace of spade. I'll postpone the fight as long as you need. He's not going anywhere, but don't drag it out."

"I'll need to train and that could take a while."

"Okay. I'll be checking on you."

Chapter Five
Fighting Johnny

Four weeks after the fight, Johnny has slowly started back training. His ribs still hurt, but he dealt with the pain. He punched the hay bales with his work gloves until the soreness went away.

In the mornings, he ran and jumped the fence before he started his three-mile run. In the afternoons, he does sit-ups and pushups until he collapses. Joey came in from school and watched Johnny exercise.

Joey said, "I can't do but one or two of them pushups and you do over a hundred."

"As you get older, you'll be able to do more."

The following week, Rizer came by to see how Johnny is doing. "When are you going to be able to fight?"

"In another week. I'm not completely healed, but I think I'll be ready."

"Good, I'll make the final arrangements."

The night of the fight came. Rizer and Johnny rode to a black community. "Are we the only white people here?"

"That's right."

"Are you sure this is wise on our part?"

They pulled up into a parking lot at a dance club. "Johnny says, there must be fifty black people here and the two of us. I don't like this."

"They're not going to fool with us. The white establishment allows them to operate without an alcohol license if they stay in their part of town and keep their problems under control. Besides, there are whites that know we're here and I got a pistol on me."

When they got out of the automobile, the thin six-feet, four-inch owner, Darnell, of the establishment came out with the fighter, Clayborn. Darnell shook Rizer and Johnny's hand. Johnny looked at his opponent and he looked mad as hell.

The stars are out on this forty-degree night. Johnny looks at the north star and hopes it brings him luck since he's admired it for all his life. Both the fighters keep their underwear top on for the fight.

Rizer raised his hand and dropped it for the fight to start. Clayborn came out swinging with Johnny evading the attack. Clayborn stopped for a few seconds before coming at his adversary again. Johnny sidestepped the attack, but his enemy attempted to tackle him. Johnny gave him a right and a left to the side of the head preventing him from going down. Clayborn launched another attack, but Johnny knocked him to the ground and got on top and began to punch down on his foe. Once Darnell had seen enough, he threw in the towel and Johnny got up, but Clayborn continued to swing at Johnny. Darnell and another man grabbed hold of him to stop the fight. Johnny stood watching as the rabid Clayborn wanted to continue fighting.

Darnell said to Rizer, "I throwed the towel in too

early. How about letting them go at again?"

Rizer said, "No. The fight is over and I'm taking all of the money as agreed."

Darnell stepped in front of him to prevent him from taking another step. "I say we split the pot."

Rizer says, "You're the one that threw in the towel. Why should I give you anything?"

"I made a mistake. My man had a lot of fight left in him. You know that."

"I'll give you ten percent of the purse to cover any expenses. Take it or leave it."

Darnell stares into the steely-eyed Rizer. "Alright, but I want a rematch."

"We'll see about that. Here's seventy-five dollars."

Rizer and Johnny took off in the Coupe.

Johnny said, "You've got a set of balls on you to pull off what you did."

"He threw the towel in and he knew he was to blame. You would've beat that nigger's ass anyway. Congratulations on the win."

"Thanks. What now?"

"I'll get us another fight soon enough. How do you feel?"

"I feel alright."

Rizer dropped Johnny off and handed him $600. "That will add to your stash. I bet you haven't spent any of your prior winnings."

"I haven't had a chance—being bedridden and training."

The next morning, Johnny handed his father $150 and got a surprise look in return. Johnny began plowing the field up for a spring garden.

Joey helped him when he got in from school in the afternoons. "Johnny, will you come to school and straighten out some boys?"

"Whose giving you problems?"

"Quincy Major's son and two of his friends."

"What have they done to you?"

"They hold me and hit me in the stomach at lunch when the teacher isn't looking. They're always tripping me and calling me names."

"What kind of names?"

"Cracker boy—White trash—Stupid—Bastard. All the kids think there's something wrong with me."

"I'll be up there and talk to Mrs. Gray tomorrow at lunch. I'll make sure I can get the wagon from Daddy."

The next day, Johnny goes to work with his father, and he'll ride to the school for the lunch period.

He's sat out in the front of the schoolhouse when they came out for lunch leaving Mrs. Gray by herself inside. Joey came out to greet him and the girls remembered him from the previous years. They wanted to talk to him, but he had eyes on the three little bullies. The three punks looked at him and turned their head.

He went inside and said, "Hello, Mrs. Gray."

She replied, "Hello, Johnny. What brings you up here today?"

"Well, Joey was telling me the Major kid and a couple of his cohorts have been giving him a hard time. What do you know of this?"

She looked down at her desk and responded, "Shouldn't his parents be up here?"

"No. I have to look out for Joey."

"Johnny, I know the boys pick on him as others have picked on a few throughout the years. I will not let it get out of hand. You know my tenure here as a teacher that doesn't allow children to misbehave in the classroom. Everyone must have a chance to learn and Joey is slow compared to the other children his age to be honest with you."

"With kids picking on him, I can believe that is affecting his learning."

"Well, Johnny, all I can tell you is that I'll continue to work with him at his ability and I'll begin punishing the boys for misbehavior."

"I appreciate that, but I've got something to say to those boys."

Johnny walked out and Mrs. Gray followed him outside. He went directly to the three punks.

He stood over the eight-year-old boys and said, "Look at me you little turds, you keep your hands-off Joey and don't be calling him names anymore because next time I come up here for any of that nonsense, I'm going to pull your heads off. Do you hear me?"

They nodded their heads. He knelt down to them and said, "I want to hear you say it. Now, say it."

The only one that doesn't verbally respond is the Quincy boy. Johnny got mad and grabbed the kid by the hair and said, "I didn't hear you, boy."

"Yes. I heard you."

"You better do more than just hear!"

Johnny got up and walked to the wagon with Mrs. Gray following him.

When he mounted the wagon, she said, "You let your anger get the best of you. Do you realize what you created with the Majors?"

"No more than what's been going on since I first saw them rednecks."

He rode back to work came home, and Johnny was just getting in from work. "How did your day go, Joey?"

"It went good after you scared the wits out of them boys."

"Good. If anything, else happens, let me know."

The next day, Rizer drove up and Johnny walked out to meet him. "I've got another fight lined up for you."

So, Johnny continued to fight once a month and never loses.

He bought himself a horse with some of his winnings.

December 1941 came and Rizer drove up and Johnny walked out to meet him.

"Who you got me pitted against this time—King Kong?"

"I haven't seen the nigger yet, but nigger Darnell says he's big."

"That's not good."

"You'll do fine. Did you know the United States declared war on Japan after they attacked Pearl Harbor in Hawaii?"

"No. I didn't. Why did Japan attack the U.S.?"

"It is all part of a big plan."

Johnny thought about that and realized it's beyond his realm of knowledge.

How about the fight taking place in one week from this Saturday?"

"No. I've been fighting a lot in the past several months. I'll need more time to rest and get strong again."

"I'll see if nigger Darnell's fighter will hold off for a while. I'll be back to check on you next week."

William rode up after Rizer has departed.

"How was your day, Johnny?"

"I can't complain."

"Did the Majors cause any problems?"

"You know how they are. They'll pop up soon enough."

"That's what I worry about."

"Rizer said the United States and Japan are at war."

"Yeah. I heard that. Is Rizer wanting you to fight again?"

"That's what he wants, but I told him I need a break in fighting."

"Is that all that fella does? Does he have a real job?"

"I've never asked him about his personal life. He lets out bits of information sometimes. He said the war is part of a plan."

"How would he know about such things?"

"I don't know. He thinks I'm kind of a white superman."

"He's right about that."

"He thinks I can be something important."

"Hmm. How will that happen?"

"By fighting."

"That's a long shot, Johnny. Quincy roughed you up and there's hundreds of people like him all over this country."

"He thinks because I'm young, I'll grow into this superman."

"You may do it."

It's late February 1942, Johnny has been seeing one of his female ex-classmates, Susan, for some time and he spent time with her in the evenings. Before he goes to see her late one afternoon, Rizer came by.

"Are you ready for another fight, Johnny?"

"Not really, but what have you got?"

"Nigger Darnell has got another big nigger for you to fight."

"Alright — the Saturday following this Saturday."

Johnny came in late, the Friday before the fight, after seeing his Susan. The following morning, Johnny woke up late with Joey staring at him.

"Good morning Joey. What's up this morning?"

"What are we going to be doing today?"

"Not much. I'm going to be resting a lot today. I'm going for a run this morning after I eat something. Would you like to ride alongside me?"

"Sure."

His mother wanted to cook him some eggs, but he doesn't want her to cook extra for him. He ate some leftover bacon and a biscuit with a glass of milk. Him and Joey went out to the barn and milked the three cows.

Johnny said, "You can take Gypsy or my horse, Red, if you like. I'll meet you out on the road. I'm going to cut across the field."

Joey responded, "Oh boy. I'm going to watch you jump that fence."

They met out on the road and talked as they traveled on the road.

"Johnny, do you think I'll ever be able to do the things you do?"

"Put all you got into it and you'll be able to do a lot of things. How's school going and tell me the truth, not just what you think I want to hear."

"It's going okay."

"Has Mrs. Gray been teaching you anything?"

"She has."

"What about the Major boy and his buddies?"

"They don't like me, but they don't bother me anymore."

"That's a good thing. Always keep your wits about you when the Majors are around. They're the meanest bunch in the county."

They traveled a way before Joey asked, "We haven't looked at the stars in a while. When do you want to watch them again?"

"How about tomorrow night?"

"That will be fun. Have you got another fight tonight?"

"How did you know?"

"You change things up when you fight."

"Yeah. I guess everyone around here knows."

When they got back home, Joey brought Red to the barn to unsaddle him and placed him into the pasture. Johnny went inside the house and saw his mother crying at the table. He walked over and saw a piece of paper in front of her.

"What's wrong Momma?"

"Ooh Johnny. It's real bad news."

Johnny looked down on the paper and sees his name on it. "What is that with my name on it?"

She tried to gather herself to tell him, "They're drafting you into the military. You've got to report in two weeks."

"Does that mean I'm going to the wars."

"I'm afraid so. I don't want you to go."

"What if I don't go?"

"They'll send men looking for you."

"They'll find me if I stay here and I ain't got nowhere else to go."

"Ooh Johnny. What are we going to do?"

"I don't really have a choice. I'll go and help win the war for the United States."

He leaves her crying at the table and walks outside. Joey sees him and walks over to see what he's doing.

"You're white as a sheet. What's wrong, Johnny?"

"Bad news."

"What is it?"

He hesitated on what to say. "I'll tell you tomorrow night while we're watching the stars."

"I hope I can wait that long. Can you give me a hint?"

"Tomorrow night. I'm going to lie down."

"Can I come lie down with you?"

"Yes. Come on."

Johnny lay on his back and Joey lay beside him with his arm wrapped around his brother. Johnny stared at the ceiling contemplating his past, present, and future. "What will become of him," he thinks? Joey watched the troubled eyes, wide opened, of Johnny.

Joey asked, "Are you going to sleep?"

"I doubt that will happen."

"You're upset about that bad news."

"Yeah, I am, but there's nothing I can do about it."

"I wish you would tell me."

"In time. Let's just rest for now."

They get up and walk around the property and they return to lie down again. They repeat it until darkness comes. It's a cool night and Johnny doesn't know what to expect at the fight. It's as if his brain has been removed. He feels empty inside.

Rizer dove up and picked up Johnny.

Johnny said, "I got a draft notice today and I have to report in two weeks from Monday."

Rizer responded, "You win this fight tonight and I'll try to get you out of that draft notice."

"You will?"

"Yes. I know some people that can help you out."

Johnny started thinking about winning the fight no matter how big his opponent will be.

Chapter Six
Tough Times

They drove up at Darnell's club and there's at least seventy-five people waiting in the parking lot. Johnny and Rizer shakes Darnell's his hand and looked at his fighter. He is an impressive man at six-feet-four-inches, two-hundred-thirty-pounds and built like a black Herculean twin.

Johnny looked at Rizer and asked, "Had you met or asked about this beast of an opponent?"

Rizer says, "I'm afraid I just took Darnell's word."

"That's unfortunate. This guy looks like he could beat his way out of a metal building."

"You've proved yourself to me too many times to get worried now."

Rizer introduced the fighters and released them to fight. Johnny took his precautionary fight beginning, but big Howard stalked but doesn't jab or swing. Johnny realized the big buck had been informed of his fighting techniques. He knew he's against the wall with a most probable superior fighter. He was backed against the crowd with nowhere to go but fight and fight he does. He came out swinging, but Howard blocked the punches and gave a right and left cross, which Johnny avoided by leaning backwards. He realized he's fighting a man with a lot of experience that is above his level. The big Howard realized he has the experience, size, and probably power over his smaller opponent. He continued to stalk Johnny until he slammed a body shot into him when he attempted to evade him. That opened-up for a right and left cross that knocked Johnny backwards. He is dazed and continues to elude him until another body shot landed and a piece of uppercut grazed his chin. He's having a hard time catching his breath as the larger and more powerful foe closed in for the finish.

Suddenly, Johnny found himself lying on the ground and the sky is spinning above him.

He heard, "He's done for man. It's over."

He saw Howard slipping his shirt over his bulging muscles. He sat up and saw Rizer handing Darnell a roll of money after he took his share. Rizer extended his hand down to Johnny. He accepted the help up.

They walked to the vehicle and got in. Rizer says, "Don't take this defeat too personal. I didn't do my research on Howard. I heard someone in the crowd say he was a heavyweight boxer from Cleveland and that he couldn't get any professional bouts because the fight game was rigged against him for being black. He has been picking up hundred-dollar fights across the country. So, you may've just fought the real heavyweight champion of the world. Too bad. Quincy Major would've probably matched up against him better."

"Quincy couldn't have beat that guy. He so outclassed me. I never had a chance to be honest. I guess this ends my fighting career."

"Well, I've got to keep searching for the great white

hope. You had a good run, but it usually ends in a similar fashion."

On the way home, Johnny realized there will not be any last-minute saving him from the war. He got a 'good luck' from Rizer and then he takes off to never be seen again.

Johnny felt his nose was broken as he walks to the house. The lights was off, and everyone seemed to be asleep.

When he got to his bed, Joey asks, "Did you win again?"

"No."

"I bet you almost won."

"Joey, I'd rather not talk about it. It's been a long tough day. Goodnight, Joey."

"Goodnight, Johnny. You are my favorite person in the whole wide world."

"Thanks, Joey. I love you.

"I love you too."

The next morning at breakfast, William told his son, "I heard the bad news about having to report to the Army. I don't know how long this war business will go on. I was told that Germany has already conquered a large portion of those European countries and Japan has spread into Southeast Asia. I don't know what that really means, but it doesn't sound good at all."

"It sounds like I need to go fight. They probably need every man they can get."

"I wish I knew what to tell you. I see your nose is swollen. How did it go last night?"

"Not good. They brought a big black professional

heavyweight down from Cleveland. I wasn't any match for him."

"That's hard to believe."

Johnny was silent as he ate and so was everyone at the table.

As the days trickled away, Johnny attempted to not dwell on his upcoming departure, but it was not ever very far from his thoughts. All the family tried to spend as much time with him as they can. His mother attempted to make his last days on the farm as pleasant as possible. His father turned down jobs to be near his son. Joey followed Johnny everywhere when he's not in school.

And then the day comes, Joey cries before going to school and leaving his brother for an indefinite period. He tells Johnny, "Please come back as fast as you can. I don't have anybody but you." He rides away on Red and looks back until Johnny is out of sight.

His mother cries as she hands him a knapsack of food and a picture of her and him. His father stops the wagon at the bus station in Woodville, Texas. His father and mother sit with him at the station until it's time for him to depart. They hug and kiss him before he gets on the bus. He walks onto the bus and in a few minutes, he is headed for boot camp at Fort Hood near Killeen, Texas.

The long bus ride provided Johnny time to think about the past two weeks—how it went

so fast with such an effect on his life. It was laid out and occurred as if it was destiny. Now, he is on a new journey without expectations. The only thing he knew is that it will be difficult. How difficult, he does not know.

He saw several other young men on the bus. He believed they are on the same journey as himself. Johnny rested on the bus until it arrives in Killeen after midnight. They are mentally and physically tested before being accepted into the Army. An Army bus awaited them there where they loaded up and are taken to the base.

Once they arrive, a Sergeant began yelling for them to get off the bus and lineup in front of him. Most knew what to do but not Johnny until he saw them lineup in single file. He fail in and they marched to the barbers to have their haircuts. After the haircuts, they marched them to the Quartermaster distribution center. The Quartermaster personnel handed out the allotted items to each new draftee. They rushed the draftees through the process with a couple of sergeants yelling to the top of their lungs at them.

Johnny hurried as do the other young men taking orders from the sergeants. They are ordered to do double time to the barracks they are assigned. There is already young men standing at attention by their bunk when the new arrivals came in and are assigned their bunks. They fall into attention for another hour before Staff Sergeant Class Romano comes before the company and picks out certain individuals for squad leaders. He fills the positions with minorities from the group—Italians, Mexicans, and Puerto Ricans. These selected leaders are assigned recruits to take care of the barracks, latrine, and other cleaning assignments.

Romano was a slightly overweight man with balding black hair and black eyes covered with eyeglasses. He talked smooth without yelling. Johnny felt he had hatred for whites because he never talked to any of them. He let his squad leaders do the dirty work for him. He intended to have the best company in the brigade which would help raise his rank to Tech Sergeant or even First Sergeant. To ensure himself to have the best company in the brigade, he had his squad leaders get the men up two to three hours earlier than designated. This allowed more time for training by being first in and out of the chow hall.

Drill Sergeant Buscemi was an Italian of small size, five-feet-six-inches tall and 150 pounds. To him, the men are to obey orders and nothing else should be said—whining will not be tolerated. He is in great physical condition and pushes the company beyond their limits except for Johnny and a few conditioned athletes.

After evening chow and everyone has showered, Johnny and his squad must clean the shower room and latrine. Most are in bed by 2200, but Johnny could be up until 0030 and during service week they must rise at 0230—normal mornings are 0330 to ensure they are first for chow. They close off all the toilets, urinals, and lavatories except for three each for 80 men. The lines are long, and the wait is long with absolutely no privacy.

Romano is the culprit for this abuse, and it doesn't end there. One night, Sergeant Buscemi pulled a drunk and comes into the barracks at 0100 and throws a large trash can between a row of bunks. He started yelling for them to 'pop tall.' They rose to attention by their bunks and he had them do 1300 side-straddle hops and then he departed.

The next morning Romano informed everyone that

he is sorry, and it will not happen again. Johnny believed Romano was in on it with Buscemi.

With Johnny's tight schedule, he gets only 3-4 hours of sleep per night. When he marches, he is half a sleep. He keeps going only by instinct.

During service week, he worked one twelve-hour day in the spud locker—peeling and cutting up potatoes. The remainder of the week, he gets lucky by being assigned to the officer's mess hall. He cleans the floor, tables, and ensures all the beverage machines are replenished. Also, he can eat from the officer's choices, which makes Johnny happy since the recruit mess hall serves only distasteful food and sugared doughnuts for dessert—the same instant food day after day— powdered eggs and powdered milk.

One of his instructors sees him in the officer's mess hall at lunch time. "How is it going, Holland?" he asks.

Johnny is surprised that he remembers his name. "Sir, things are doing good while I work in here this week."

The short strong-built instructor asks him, "Where are you from?"

"Texas, sir."

"Things will get better when you leave here unless you get caught in one of those POW (prisoner of war) camps. Nice talking to you, Holland."

"Thank you, sir."

Johnny felt good that someone in this damn army treats him with some respect.

Once the company attained the number one company in the brigade, Romano allows the company, for the last few days of their training, to proceed on regular recruit hours. Johnny writes his mother as often as he can, and she always writes back.

But Romano's wickedness does not end. Since the food from the chow hall is so disgusting, he'll bring in hamburgers, from the outside, for the company if they pitch in $2 each for one. Johnny gets his hamburger as one of the last in the company because of his cleaning duties. The two pieces of bread and thin slice of meat is cold. The next day, Romano gets $3 for a plate of spaghetti, but the spaghetti runs out before Johnny can make it to eat. Romano is nowhere to be found. His selected minorities can only tell him, "I don't know what to tell you."

The next day, the greedy Romano wants $2 from each for another hamburger. Johnny told the squad leader to kiss his ass. The squad leader wanted to press charges, but the leader of squads let it die. Tomorrow is the graduation of the brigade and he wanted it clear of problems. Johnny realizes Romano profited nearly $500 on the desperation of the hungry recruits, but only his selected few got their stomachs full.

The graduation went well as a Major inspected the brigade. Before lunch, the recruits receive their orders and are on their way home for furlough. He rides the bus home with relief after the agonizing past two months.

He walked the nine miles from town to his home. When he arrived, it was early afternoon and his mother was the only one to greet him.

"If we would've known, your father and I would have met you in town."

"The craziness of the Army doesn't allow you to know such things. How is Joey and all of you?"

"We are doing okay. We've missed you so much.

How are you?"

"I just need a few days of rest and good food and I'll be ready to go."

"You'll get that, Johnny. I can promise you that."

Joey comes home and sees Johnny waiting for him at the barn. "Johnny, Johnny, I knew you would be back."

He jumps from his horse and jumps on Johnny. Johnny holds and kisses him.

"How are things with you, Joey?"

"It hasn't been too bad. I missed you a whole bunch."

"I missed you more than you can imagine. It was a tough undertaking."

"Can we watch the stars tonight?"

"Of course, we can."

Joey saw William riding up. "I'll see you after while, Johnny."

He came in from working at a neighboring farm. "Johnny, I can't believe you're here. How are you, son?"

"I could be better, but I'm here now and that's a good thing."

"You bet. I want you to tell me what they had you doing since I never was in the military."

"I can't say much of it was good. They break your spirit and make you live with it."

"That's because when you get off in them foreign countries in bad times, you won't be so down when all hell breaks loose."

"Maybe so."

Johnny assisted his father with unloading the

wagon of tools. "Guess what about the Majors? C.R. got drafted and Willard joined the Navy."

"That's two that won't be bothering you."

"You know, I haven't seen or heard from that bunch for quite a while. I heard the news about C.R. and Willard from a man down the road."

"They're a no-account bunch that you always need to keep your eyes and ears open for."

"Yep, I know that. How long are you going to be with us?"

"Ten days and I'll return to Fort Hood for training in a tank destroyer battalion. Then, I'll be shipped off overseas."

"Tank destroyer that sounds like a rough job."

"It probably will be."

The conversation continued until supper. Johnny enjoyed his mother's cooking and the family talking. Even Joey wasn't afraid to talk with Johnny now there.

That night, Johnny and Joey go and lie on top of the haystack and gaze at the stars.

Joey asks, "Are these the same stars you had at that fort?"

"Yep. It's the same stars."

"What do you think is on them stars?"

"I don't know, but I think there's people out there on some of the stars."

"You said that before. Do you think they look like us?"

"Maybe. I would like to know."

"I would, too. Would you be scared if they don't look like us?"

"I might be."

It became quiet except for the locusts buzzing for a

couple of minutes.

"What did they make you do at that fort?"

"Clean and train."

"What do you mean clean and train?"

"I cleaned toilets, showers, and floors. I trained in marching, studying all kind of stuff, and lots of other things."

"I don't understand."

"Hopefully, you never will."

Chapter Seven
Off to War

Johnny went to see Susan the second evening he is in. Once he talked a few minutes to her parents, he and her go riding on Red.

She hung on tight to Johnny's hard mid-section. "I've missed you, Johnny."

"I missed you too and thought about you every day."

Johnny takes a cutoff to the creek. "Do you want to go to the creek? It's been a hot day."

"I'll go wherever you want."

They rode to the creek and got off Red and started kissing. Within a few minutes, they are lying on the sand and getting intimate. It is becoming dark as she lies her upper half on his upper body.

The dark-haired seventeen-year-old asked, "Do you like the Army?"

"No."

"I've heard mixed things about it. Why didn't you join the Navy? My uncle retired from it. He liked it and now gets a pension."

"Well, I didn't really think about joining anything else. If the Army wanted me, I should at least try them. Anyway, I wouldn't like being out on a tin can being shot at. You have nowhere to go. You just go down with the ship."

"I just thought I would mention it since you don't like the Army."

The military isn't my thing. When the Army is finished with me, I'll be out of there."

"I wished you didn't have to go back. We could just lie around the creek or wherever and have fun."

"You have one more year of school and what are you going to do?"

"I'm not going to worry about it until I have to."

They became intimate again.

Johnny spent his days and nights at home, but his evenings are with Susan. He is falling for her and she has already fallen for him.

He was already thinking of his mandatory return to the Army, but he's enjoyed every minute of being home. When he returned home from seeing Susan, he and Joey lie on the grass and watched the cosmos until midnight.

Joey watched as his Mother can't keep her hands-off Johnny and his father wanted him near all the time. Joey can't understand the huge disparity of how Johnny is treated and himself. He has a lifetime of pain and he is just ten years old.

Johnny done his best to spread his time with everyone as his last few days wind down.

The last day of his leave came and he spent most of the night with Susan.

She says, "I'm going to write you every day. Is that alright?"

"Sure, it is, and I'll try to write you back every time."

"Do you know when you'll be back?"

"Whenever they let me."

"I hope we get married. Do you think we ever will?"

"I hope so. Let's soak in the night and hold each other."

They do while Joey waited and waited for his brother until he falls asleep.

The next morning, Johnny saw Joey was sad because he did not watch the stars with him on the last night of his leave.

"Joey, I'm sorry I didn't make it back in time last night. Remember me every time you see a falling star."

"I'll remember you all the hours I'm awake. You won't be here if I need you."

"I could show up anytime—just remember that."

"I bought something for your tenth birthday next week." He hands him a twelve-gauge pump shotgun. "Take it, but always use it carefully. You've been with me hunting and you've shot my gun. Let's go outside and try it out."

He demonstrated and instructed Joey in utilization of the gun until he felt satisfied that Joey would operate it competently.

"Can I go with you all to the train station?"

William heard the question to Johnny and responded, "You need to stay here and do your chores."

Joey looked at Johnny for support and Johnny contemplated what was said before saying anything. "Why can't he go this one day? He's not in school. There's no telling when and if I'll be back."

William said, "Don't talk like that, Johnny. You'll be back because you're going to win the war for the

United States. He can go with us this time."

After breakfast, they traveled to the train station and said their goodbyes with tears.

When he arrived this time, there was no yelling and screaming. It was a more serious environment. The following morning, he was driven to a large field away from any type of facilities. For the next few weeks, he will live in a tent and drink creek water that was purified. Food would be brought in by a truck periodically. It is a rugged training site.

The Battery Officer Captain Fredrick spoke to the new platoons. "You have been assigned to this Battalion to train as tank destroyers. I'll provide you a brief overview of what we're about. The Nazis have built the most powerful tanks in the world and they've got plenty of them. The Russians may differ on the most powerful. The Army created this battalion to act as independent units that would respond quickly to enemy tank attacks. While you're here, you'll learn every known method of tank destruction, from the massed fire of the mobile, self-propelled heavy weapons to the ambushing of tanks, guerilla-fashioned, by the individual soldier armed with Molotov cocktails and sticky grenades. Good luck here and wherever you end up."

The Platoon Leader Officers called out the members for their platoon and then are assigned to squads with sergeants in charge of each one. Johnny is assigned to Sergeant Lowery who has just returned from the 601st Battalion in North Africa. He is thirty-years old, medium height, and slightly thin.

The first day, he had them run ten miles to check

their stamina level. They did satisfactory to Sergeant Lowery, but they came in sometimes several minutes apart. Johnny was first and that provided him an edge in the Sergeant's eye. The afternoon, the Sergeant introduced them to the weaponry they would be exposed to during training.

That evening, Lowery informed the squad of the German10th Panzer Division attack at the Battle of El Guettar in North Africa. "I'll tell you about the hell hole I just came from. In North Africa, we had fifty-seven tanks attack our troops in the wide open. When it was all over, we destroyed thirty tanks and we lost twenty-four of our thirty-six M3 GMC tank destroyers. Seven M-10 tank destroyers from the 899th tank destroyer battalion were also lost in the battle. We won the battle, but it was at a heavy cost. I learned some things there and we're going to put it to use in our training here."

The next morning, the squad were training in full force. He had seen an African American platoon of tank destroyers training nearby.

When the platoons' training were completed, they were given a shoulder sleeve insignia for tank destroyers, designed to set them apart and given them pride, was a black panther crushing a tank between its jaws and encircled by the words "Seek, Strike, and Destroy."

Johnny's platoon were assigned in the Ardennes of France. They had seen effective use of tank destroyers in a mobile defense, but when they were used in a counter-attacking role, they were often knocked out or destroyed. Luckily, Johnny's squadron were still intact.

The forested area of the Ardennes were almost impenetrable, but Johnny's squadron had nestled in a secluded area after being informed of by a reconnaissance platoon. They were in wait of a German tank advance with a towed 3" M5 anti-tank gun and a M3 Halftrack with armored self-propelled guns. One of the deficiencies was no armored covering over the turret. Many men had lost their lives for that reason, but Johnny's squadron improvised by using a metallic sheeting over the turret. This deflected grenades and provided protection against overhead artillery bursts.

As Johnny and his squad waited for the approaching tank charge, he thinks of all the death he had already witnessed. Would he be the next lifeless mangled body to be found by his comrades?

As he continues to wait, he worries about Joey and how he is being treated at home and school. He and all his loved ones—Susan, Mother, Joey, and Father have been writing back and forth throughout his military duration. It keeps his hopes alive with their letters.

One soldier notice how much mail Johnny receives and says, "Would you mind if I read some of your mail? I don't have anyone that writes to me."

Johnny handed him a letter from his father. He glimpsed at the soldier as he read it and he could see the joy in the soldier's eyes.

Suddenly, they heard the German tanks moving closer and closer. They had their guns ready for the first sight of them, but how close will they be when they come upon them in the dense forest.

The tanks appeared and the tank destroyers attack with repeated fire of high velocity armored-piercing blasts incapacitating the crew inside. The squad done a remarkable job of destroying three tanks, but the proximity brought infantry and artillery attacks, and even attacks from the tanks.

They were now under attack. Another squad attempted to slow down the attack for Sergeant Lowery's squad, but the Germans propelled through any support using hand grenades and machine guns. Johnny was backing away, from the assault, by shooting his rifle—hitting the closest pursuing German soldiers. He had seen some of his fellow squad members go down from artillery shells. Their anti-tank guns were being terminated by grenades. There were many German infantrymen flanking him at every turn. He had sought cover from the onslaught of bullets in a small grove of trees. He was being overwhelmed, but he continued to pick off a shooter when he had the chance.

They had enough of him picking them off. They threw some grenades at him and knocked him out of action. The German soldiers slowly moved in his direction and found Johnny clumped over with a pile of dirt on top of him. The grenade had done in the East Texas small time legend. As the soldiers began to walk away from him, they see movement from the tough Johnny and realize he has a chance of surviving the concussion and pieces of shrapnel that ripped into his back. He is taken as a prisoner of war.

After recovering from the wounds in a prisoner of war (POW) camp, Johnny is assigned with others that were captured from his platoon. Sergeant Lowery is the only one from his squad that is in the barracks.

Lowery goes to receive Johnny. "How are you Johnny? I heard you took a direct blast from a grenade."

"I don't know how direct, but it done me in for how

long?"

"You've been in the POW infirmary for about three weeks."

"How about the others in our squad?"

"No one made it but you and me."

Johnny said, "I saw some of them killed. The Germans come upon us rather quick. Huh?"

"Yeah. We did our share of damage to the enemy but look at the cost."

"I believe we were sacrificed for what damage we did."

"We're just a small piece of the big plan regarding this war. You have to accept that, or you'll go mad."

"I'm already mad. I've got to get out of here or the madness will grow."

"Calm down. You just got out of the infirmary and we get exercise daily. You need to get your body working normal again. In the meantime, we'll have time to think on this escape."

Chapter Eight
POW

As the weeks go by, Johnny's body had recuperated well, but the only thing own his mind was escape. He talked to Sergeant Lowery every day and he informed him of his plan.

Johnny says, "Since you seem okay in allowing these Nazis to control every move you make, I've decided that I'm going to jump that fence and get the hell out of here."

"How do you expect to jump a ten-foot fence and escape the guards and dogs?"

"I can jump to that ten-foot wire and pull myself over and be out of here as quick as you can walk to the latrine."

"Have you thought this out in anyway?"

"I discovered a dark spot between two buildings that I've studied and can make a quick run from for the fence between the watch light."

"I know you are a good athlete, but you are underestimating that fence. It will not be as easy as you think with three wires to climb over. You get hung on that fence for more than a minute, they'll shoot you dead. You're not thinking right, Johnny. All you can think of is getting out of here."

"My strength is starting to fade with the food and rations they give us. Everyday, I'll grow weaker. I've thought it out and if I don't go now, my chances will get lower as time goes by."

"I don't like it, Johnny."

"I would rather be dead than be in here another day. Tonight, I'm out of here."

The sergeant didn't want Johnny to attempt his escape, but he knows Johnny will never wait out the ongoing war.

Later that night, Johnny made his way from the barracks and waited between the buildings for the count of the light beam cycle. He had seen a guard with two big German Shepard dogs. He surely didn't want them being too close.

When Johnny thought things were aligned for him to go, he attempted the jump. He grabbed it with both hands, but the wire shook for several yards from his grasp. The dogs sensed it and that brought the guard's attention to it.

Johnny attempted to pull himself over the wire, but his strength seemed to be lacking for the feat. He had his chin to the wire, but suddenly, he heard and felt the vicious clutches of the German Shepard dogs latching onto his buttock and leg. He continued to pull, but the weight of the dogs and the light beaming on him, he dropped from the traumatic aftermath. The dogs continued to maul him until the guard sees he's done. He pulled the ferocious dogs off him and called for assistance.

Johnny was chewed from head to toe. The large dogs would have killed him if the guard had allowed them to finish the attack. The Nazis throw him in the hoe with limited medical treatment.

Sergeant Lowery and many of the POWs heard about Johnny's attempted escape. They worried about him surviving in the hole with the wounds incurred.

Johnny suffered tremendously from his escape attempt. The shrapnel wounds had been reopened from the dogs ripping teeth. Every bite was painful and some of them were deep gashes that needed attention. During the night, he suffered from chills and fever. He was delirious and he kept running the attempted escape over and over in his mind.

The next day, he received medical attention but was left in the hole. He received bread and water rations.

After a few days, Johnny felt he was dying. He kept thinking that he was needed at home. Joey must need him. "I cannot die." He says to himself. He wished he had a letter to read that would keep his hopes alive.

When a person was in a degraded position, badly wounded, the mind in turmoil—the spirit begins to want a new body. Without hope and without a reason to live, there comes a time when the spirit cannot hold on to a lost cause any longer.

As life began to fade from Johnny, he awakens in the infirmary feeling drained and near death. After more than a week, he can finally speak more than one word at a time. When he awoke sometimes in the morning, he thought he was back home, but quickly returns to reality.

After a few weeks of being in the infirmary, he is released to light duty. He got around very slowly and was under constant surveillance.

One day, he was taken to the Nazi doctor. Dr.

Vander Gaff could speak English well but with a strong German accent. The doctor saw the frail Johnny standing in front of him. "Hello, Johnny. Sit down. I would like to talk to you for a few minutes. Are you getting better?"

"I feel I am, but I'm a long way from being what I was before being captured."

"You have survived a stressful ordeal, but without my assistance, you would not have. I had you removed from the hole because you were near death. I made sure you would survive from the dogs' attack wounds. You had a little luck on your side, but I am the one you owe your life to without a doubt."

Johnny responded, "Doctor, why did you leave me in the hole until death was upon me if you were planning to keep me alive?"

"Adversity is a test of the human spirit. I wanted to know your limit under the most horrid conditions. We perform similar tests in the laboratory quite regularly."

"What do you want from me for you saving my life. Isn't this talk all about that?"

Dr. Vander Gaff answered, "You have Aryan blood in you and that makes you worth saving, but there are conditions as you have perceived. I need information on the Allied forces that maybe helpful to our cause. There are several hundred troops here that are our prisoners. Many of them don't even know what country they are in while others have a wealth of vital information for our intelligence. Are you willing to help?"

"What alternative do I have?"

"I am afraid, there is but one alternative. You will become a participant in our research laboratory."

"Your answer must be provided at this time."

Johnny had no intention of providing any information to the evil doctor that could endanger anyone on the American side and its allies, but he must bide for time or face the lab butchers.

As the doctor looked firmly at Johnny, he asked, "How do you want me to go about this?"

Vander Gaff said, "If you are too obvious, you will be recognized as a snitch. Listen for information and inquire delicately. I will send for you in a few days and I will expect something of value. Do you understand?"

"Yes, doctor."

Vander Gaff opened the door for the guard to escort the prisoner to his old barracks. Johnny was glad to be out of the presence of the wicked doctor, but he knew his back was against the wall in a crushing way.

When the feeble Johnny showed up in his barracks, he got a standing ovation. The men honored him for the escape attempt and his determination to survive the ordeal.

Sergeant Lowery meets him with a hug and offers him a smoke. He accepts and they walk outside to sit and smoke the cigarettes.

"Johnny, you look like hell, but you're still here."

"Look at my hands and wait till you see the rest of my body. I never had a chance, Sergeant. You were right. I was too hard-headed to see I was in no condition to try that."

"You're lucky to be alive. When I heard you survived, I thought that they would execute you."

"They almost succeeded with a week in the hole."

"I'm surprised they let you out of there."

"Kind of like, divine intervention."

"God definitely had a hand in your life. I think you ought to know that we are to be transferred to a POW camp in Germany within the month."

Johnny contemplates this move with caution. "Will anybody be left here?"

"No. This was just a temporary holding camp. I think the Allies are making a strong push into the German stronghold. From what I heard, we'll be transferred by box car to some POW camps in Germany."

Meanwhile, William had worked for a man in town and was coming home that afternoon. He was a few miles from his home when old man Major and Quincy pulled up behind him in the truck and started honking the horn for him to get out of the way. William pulled over for them to get around him. They did, but old man Major slammed his breaks and turned the truck sideways just in front of William and his wagon. Old man Major had a pistol slid into the back of his pants as he stepped from the truck. Quincy walked toward William while he sat on the wagon. William knew this was serious and his shotgun was at home. His heart began to beat at a rapid pace as the Majors walked right upon him from both sides of his wagon.

"Well, well…the cracker can't go nowhere. We owe you cracker for what your son, Johnny did. It's been a long wait, but it's pay up time."

William spoke in a delicate manner, "I haven't done you people no harm and Johnny is missing in action. What could rile you up this bad?"

"Your son yanked Quincy's son by his hair and threatened him. We've been brewing about this long enough. Quincy, get him!"

William jumped from the seat to the bed of the wagon. Quincy attempted to grab him, but the wiry William took off running in the opposite direction. Old man Major pulled his pistol out and shot at him but missed the first shot. The second shot was well-aimed and dropped him with the 38-caliber pistol.

They run to the downed man. Quincy bends down and sees him breathing. "He's still alive, Pa."

"We got to make him disappear and fast. This road isn't traveled much, but it's traveled. Put him in the back of the truck and we'll take him to the old river bluff. I got to cover up this blood while you do that."

They left William's wagon on the side of the road. As they drove off, Quincy saw William attempting to climb out of the truck. When the truck was stopped, William fell off the back of the truck. Old man Major got out of the truck and pulled his gun out and shot William point blank in the head.

"Now, he won't be falling out of the back of the truck."

Quincy loaded him in the back of the truck, and they drove him to the old river bluff where they dumped him in a secluded swamp hole and covered him with brush.

Old man Major said with disgust, "Now, the cracker is turtle and gator bait."

Lillian waited for her husband until the early morning hours of the next day, but he wouldn't be showing up ever again.

Chapter Nine
Hardships

Johnny knew he had to bide his time until the transfer, but that could be several weeks from now. He had to extract some irrelevant information without giving a name. The transfer brought about doubts if there was a laboratory doing experiments on the Allied troops. Maybe the doctor lied, but that did not mean he would be absent from torture.

He listened to everything he heard with very little that could help his cause. The next day passed and the next without the doctor sending for him. Inevitably, he is sent to see the doctor.

Vander Gaff sat down when Johnny is brought into see him. "What have you got for me, Johnny?"

"I didn't hear much, but I did hear there's an onslaught of tanks coming this way."

"I already knew about that and I am sure you heard of the transfer. You are running out of time, Johnny."

"Are you going to kill me if I don't bring something useful?"

"You will suffer a long brutal death, Johnny. Now, I will expect something useful by tomorrow. Do you understand?"

"I understand, Dr. Vander Gaff."

Johnny was escorted back to the barracks. The

whole time he was suffering from the fear instilled in him by the doctor. He hated the doctor for doing this to him and he would reach out for help.

When he got in the barracks, he went straight to Sergeant Lowery. "I need to speak to you in private, Sergeant."

"Let's go outside and smoke one."

They do and Lowery asked, "What's on your mine, Johnny?"

"I'm done Sergeant. That Dr. Vander Gaff is threatening me to tell him some intelligence or he's going to torture me to death."

"That bastard doesn't comply with the Geneva Convention. Why did he pick you out?"

"He saved my life after I suffered in that hole for a week with those dog bites."

"I've got to think about how to get you out of this."

It was quiet for a few minutes before Lowery said, "Tell him that you have no information because the Allied Forces are on top of them and he needs to flee before he's the one going to be tortured since he has broken the Geneva Convention."

"Johnny responded, "That might be the final nail in my coffin."

"You don't have any intelligence to reveal. I'm just telling you what I'd tell him."

"I'll do it, but I probably won't be seeing you again."

Lowery responded, "You don't really have a choice. Do you?"

"I guess not."

Meanwhile, back home, Joey asked his mother,

"Where is father?"

"He didn't return last night."

Joey asked out of curiosity. His father rarely talked to him and Joey knew the hate his father had against him. He just didn't know why.

Joey was at school when a neighbor told Lillian that they believed the wagon on the road belonged to her husband. Lillian went with the neighbors to check on the wagon and once she saw it was William's wagon, she rode it home. While she didn't love William anymore, she was worried about him.

As the days passed, Lillian decided William would probably not be coming home. She went to the Sheriff Gentry's office and filed a missing person report. The Sheriff ruled out robbery since all of William's tools were still in the back of the wagon.

One afternoon, Joey asked his Mother, "Is Father ever coming back?"

"Sheriff Gentry is trying to find out. Right now, he doesn't know anything except William left work at 3 PM and the wagon was spotted an hour later where it was when I drove it home the next day."

Joey said, "I think the Majors had something to do with it."

Lillian is silent for a minute before she spoke. "Is Quincy Major's son still picking on you?"

"Not anymore. I beat his butt."

"Good for you. How did you do that after all of these years of him picking on you?"

"I practiced like Johnny did. I beat that hay bale until it was in pieces. I did pushups and sit-ups until I couldn't do anymore."

Lillian said, "I sure hope Johnny comes back from

the war. I miss him dearly."

"He'll be back. I know he will."

Lillian had a feeling that Joey was right about the Majors having something to do with William's disappearance. She would tell the sheriff, but she knew there could be consequences, especially since she would now have to become the breadwinner of the family.

All day, Johnny worried about his next meeting with the doctor. He tried to think of something to appease him for further delay. Nothing was heard from the doctor the next day. He breathed easy as nightfall came. He slept better that night than the night before, but it was still somewhat of a restless night.

The next day came and it became official that they would be transferred to a prison camp in Germany within the next two weeks. Everyone was angry about the transfer except Johnny. He wanted to be transferred right now, but he was taken to the doctor by German guards.

Johnny's heart was beating rapidly, and he could see it twitching through his shirt. He had lost his bravery and his spirit was hanging on by a thread.

Vander Gaff looked at the thin Johnny as he entered his office. "Johnny, I am giving you an opportunity to save your life. You can stay here and be killed or join our cause. You will be fed and exercised like a real German soldier before being shipped out to fight on one of our fronts. What do you say to that option?"

"When will I be killed?"

"As soon as the Allies are sent to Germany. You and certain others will be hanged and left for the advancing

Allied Forces to find when they enter this vacant camp."

Johnny decided to wait it out. "I'm not joining your forces. So, that means I'll be hanged."

Nearly a minute passed before the doctor spoke. "All of this will not matter by this time next year in 1945. We will have lost the war."

"If you're so sure, why hang me?"

"It is my duty to serve Germany until the bitter end."

"Your Germany wouldn't like one of its doctors to be saying that the war isn't winnable."

"You are so irrelevant, it does not matter what you heard me say."

"Although I'm relevant enough to hang."

The malicious Vander Gaff said to the guard. "Take him to the holding cells."

Johnny glanced at the doctor on the way out, but the doctor doesn't take his eyes off the papers in front of him.

He is taken to a where three small buildings are enclosed in a double-fenced-in area. Two guard dogs roamed the enclosed area and two Nazi watches stood guard.

There, he was brought in one of the buildings. The sad faces of the prisoners already in there tell the story of their fate. Once he was alone with them, one of them inquires, "Brother, what brings you in here where a certain death awaits us within days?"

Johnny said, "I had the wrong doctor."

"The Corporal said, "This place is the entrance to hell. The Lord has forgotten us because we are part of this merciless war."

Another prisoner said, "There's no Lord or God.

Why would he have ever created such a monstrous bunch as the Nazis?"

"Satan works against our Lord, but in the end, he'll prevail."

Johnny asked, "What have you all done that got yourselves in here?"

The prisoner, that spoke before the Corporal, said, "We were sent to this miserable war."

The Corporal said, "I told the Nazis more than once that they were warriors from hell. They looked at me as a problem and they're going to get rid of me. The others were insubordinate in one way or another according to these Nazi devils. It doesn't matter since we are all doomed."

Johnny doesn't care to hear anymore from his fellow prisoners. He sat down and became quiet. He just stared at the floor as most of the others were doing.

At home, Lillian told Sheriff Gentry that she believed the Majors had something to do with William's disappearance. The sheriff didn't seem surprised since he knew of the rift at the fight a few years ago.

Sheriff Gentry saw Thomas Major in town and asked him, "Thomas, have you seen William Holland lately?"

"No. Why should I watch for him?"

"I figured since you didn't like him, you may have taken it a step further."

"What are you trying to say?"

"I say you had something to do with Thomas Major's disappearance."

"You're crazy. I don't know anything about

him."

"I'm coming out to your place and see what your hiding."

"Come on. You ain't gonna find anything."

The sheriff drove out to Thomas Major's place and Thomas followed him. "Do I need to get a search warrant, Thomas?"

Thomas replied, "No. I don't have anything to hide."

After a half-day search of the two-hundred acres and structures, the sheriff said to Thomas, "Well, I don't see anything that draws my attention, but I'd like to take an inventory of your guns."

Thomas didn't like it and was hesitant to grant the request, but he didn't want the sheriff to realize he may be hiding something. "Come on and see what I got."

After the inventory, the sheriff asked, "What about that handgun I've seen you carry around?"

"My thirty-eight is in my truck."

"Oh. I forgot about checking your vehicle."

Thomas opened the door to his truck and reached behind the seat to pull out the holstered pistol. The sheriff looked inside the truck while Thomas pulled the gun out. He saw some spent cartridges behind the seat.

He asked Thomas, "Do you always throw your casings behind the seat?"

The sheriff pulled out three casings from behind the seat.

Thomas said, "There's no telling how long they've been back there."

"I'll take him into my office in case the rest of it shows up somewhere."

Thomas asked, "Why are you going to all this trouble for a piece of white trash?"

The sheriff gave him a stern look and said, "Do you ever look in the mirror, Thomas?"

"How can you say that about me after seeing what I got and done? My two boys serving in that war over there. Quincy and Josh turning out to be good men."

"You wouldn't have had what you got if it wasn't for your pa leaving the place to you. William worked jobs all over this county to pay for his place. By the way, Johnny Holland was serving in that war and now, he's missing in action."

Thomas shook his head in disbelief because he doesn't understand why the sheriff can't see it his way. The sheriff drove back to town.

For the next few days, Johnny and his comrades waited their fate. Johnny thinks of a way to fight back, but his condition is poor to fair. Even in his miserable condition, he doesn't want to walk out and just let them hang him. He must get the others to fight with him when they come to execute them.

Johnny said loudly, "Listen everyone, are you just going to allow them to lead you to the gallows and hang you?"

Everyone is quiet until one of the prisoners said, "You're right. They're going to kill us anyway. We ought not to make it any easier for them."

The corporal said, "Can't you see this may cause a backlash for the not condemned prisoners? We must be the ones to be sacrificed."

Johnny said, "The doctor told me we would be executed when the other prisoners are being shipped off. They'll be in too much of a hurry to execute any others since the Allies are closing in on them. I say we overtake them when they come to get us. How many prisoners are there in the other two buildings?"

A Private First Class (PFC) spoke up, "There are about the same in each of the three buildings."

Johnny said, "If we could get word to them somehow, they could help us."

Sergeant Peterman spoke up, "Since I'm the highest rank in here. I think I can organize this more effective than you all can. It's my responsibility anyway. They bring them outside for a few minutes a day like they do us. We'll try to get word to them through the wall when they or we are on break. We'll probably be the last building they open. I want the three most able-bodied men among us to break this door down when they open the first building."

They looked amongst one another until three were decided on. At break, the sergeant took one building and a corporal named Janis took the other. The dozen men spread out into the yard while Johnny walked around with Janis. The Nazis watched, but the Allies signaled to one another when they were watching too close. Besides, the restrained guard dogs were barking so loud at the prisoners that the Nazis didn't know who was talking to who. Peterman and Janis each leaned their back against the appropriate buildings. Johnny talked to Janis while he watched the Nazis. Janis back tapped the building with his heel of the boot twice.

He said as if he talked to Johnny, "If you can hear what I say, tap twice."

They tap twice and Janis finished his instruction for the attack on the Nazi guards. They heard but are hesitant to agree to the request.

The group are ordered back into their structure without any assurance by the others they would agree with the plan. Once inside, the group discussed what occurred.

The sergeant said, "I'm not sure if they are with us or not."

Janis said the same thing. Johnny said, "Of course, they will join us. What choice do they have?"

The sergeant said, "I hope you're right."

Janis said, "We need to carry on as if they are with us."

The sergeant responded, "We'll proceed, and we shall be ready for them."

Chapter Ten
Leave Free or Die

The train was heard throughout the camp as it loaded boxcar after boxcar of POWs. Johnny knew today was the day. The train usually was gone in an hour, but it had been at the depot for three hours. He and the others heard German spokespersons talking nonstop through loudspeakers in German and English languages. As the voices toned down from the speakers, the train began its departure.

The POWs in the building was prepared for the Nazi assassins. As they sat silently, they heard the outside fence being opened. With a very slight opening they had made in the door, they saw a group of about ten Nazis in total. One was an officer and the rest were armed with machine guns. When they began to open the doors, Sergeant Peterman gave the signal for them to go through the door and take the guns from the Nazis.

The Nazis reacted rather quickly to the attempted coup by opening their machine guns on those coming from the buildings. A few POWs had engaged the Nazis in hand to hand combat. A big farm boy, from Kansas, came out of the first structure and overpowered a Nazi—took his machine gun and shot two Nazis but was quickly shot by the officer with his Luger. Johnny jumped on the officer after the first three from his building was killed. They went to the ground, and Johnny couldn't overpower the officer as he thought. His strength had been drained, but he knew that he could not give up no matter how much spunk the officer had in him. Bullets were whizzing by as his comrades were being annihilated. As he grappled with the Nazi officer, he expected to be shot at any time, but he and the officer had fought to a standstill. The Kansas farm boy was not finished with a bullet through his shoulder. He grabbed the machine gun again and shot five of the firing Nazis. The Nazis killed half of the thirty-six Allied including the Kansas farm boy. The remainder of the Allied had cornered themselves up in a corner of their structure. The mass executioner was a Barnitzke machine gunner. He brought his machine gun in front of the structures to finish off the resisters. Johnny had hold of the Luger barrel and wouldn't let go. Luckily for Johnny, the officer was not a big man, but he was a live wire. He started yelling for help from the Nazi machine gunners.

Johnny was not what he was before, but he knew how to fight hand to hand. He rammed his elbow into the throat of the officer, which enabled him to snatch the Luger from the officer. He shot the officer through the throat. With the officer's body shielding him from view of the machine gunners, they weren't sure if their officer was dead or not. Johnny took a careful look at his adversaries and saw the Barnitzke machine gunner about to open fire. Johnny took close aim and put a bullet through the heart of the Nazi. The three remaining Nazi machine gunners opened fire on the location of Johnny. He yelled for help as the bullets struck all around him as he aimed one more time and shot another Nazi.

Sgt, Peterman saw that only two Nazis remained and yelled, "Let's finish them off. Most of the remaining eighteen charged out as Johnny felt machine gun bullets burn through his body.

When he regained consciousness, a man stands over him. He said, "I think we have a live one here. That's Johnny."

Three stood over him as he looked up. One of the POWs said, "He has two bullet wounds with one through the shoulder and another through the lung."

Another one of the three said, "Has he got a chance to make it? Two of us need to go through the camp and see what kind of medical supplies are out there. One can stand by the two that are still alive."

"Do you think there is more Nazis in the camp?"

"Probably so, but not many since they didn't come to the aid of these Nazis."

The three remaining Allies talked amongst themselves. PFC Jeffery, a young Michigan man, said, "How about me and Joe go look around while Corporal Wilson keeps an eye on these two?"

Corporal Wilson, a six-feet tall Virginian, said, "All right. You two, be careful. Work together as if you are approaching a sniper."

After loading up on guns and ammo, they took off in the direction of the main camp. Jeffery said, "Look, the two dogs that were in our camp are now running wild. I ought to shoot them mean bastards."

Joe said, "We don't need to stir things up again as long as they don't mess with us. Anyway, look who trained them mean bastards. You follow me. Give me cover. I'm going to run to that guard post. Wait a minute and then come on."

"You got it. We've nearly got it made. Let's finish the job."

Joe ran to the guard post as Jeffery watched and listened to the emptiness of the camp. After a minute, Jeffery ran to Joe as he climbed up into the empty guard post. He barely looked over the divider wall—checking for anything that may suggest more Nazis.

Joe asked Jeffery, "Do you see anything up there?"

"Yeah. I see a lot, but no people. I spotted their medical center. I'll come down and we'll go over there."

When he comes down, Joe asked, "What do you think? Are there anymore Nazis here?"

"I don't know. It looks awfully dead around here. I think we should go on over to the medical place. I'll go first."

They reached the facility and walked in with machine guns ready. The facility was almost completely empty.

Jeffery said, "It looks like they took most everything with them. This shelf has dressings of all kinds. Our two wounded can use these. Check the drawers while I look in these rooms."

They boxed up the dressings and started looking for food. After checking the building thoroughly, they returned to eat on the food that was left in the kitchen. While eating and grabbing food, they heard a noise come from behind the trash barrels in the chow hall.

Jeffery placed the knife down and picked up the machine gun. He eased into the chow hall and saw a cook attempting to get away. Jeffery yelled, "I'll shoot if you don't stop."

The cook didn't understand what he said, but he understood when Jeffery shot the ceiling over his head. He stopped with his hands up in the air. Joe frisked him and found a butcher knife in his pocket.

As Joe walked him back toward Jeffery, he said, "I wonder how many more they left behind."

Jeffery said, "He was left to feed our assassins, but they won't be coming to dinner. Now, what are we going to do with you?"

Jeffery saw the middle-aged balding cook is trembling and scared. Jeffery said, "Let's tie him up."

They tied him up, within view, while they finished raiding the kitchen. Jeffery said, "While I bring the dressings to Corporal Wilson and the wounded, you keep an eye on the cook and if any others are creeping around here. We need to get a game plan on what we must do."

Jeremy bought the dressings and some food to Wilson. Wilson asked, "Where's Joe? I heard shots."

"Joe is fine. I fired a few shots to stop a cook. We haven't seen anyone else. The place is empty except food that was left to feed our would-be assassins. How's the two wounded guys?"

"One died and the other must be awful tough because he's got plenty of scars and he lives after two bullets went through him. We'll see if we can dress his wounds without killing him."

They dressed his wounds and he talked briefly. Johnny said, "We must've won for you two to be looking down on me."

Wilson said, "I think we won. Now, if we can stay

alive until the Allied Forces get to us."

Johnny responded, "Good." He was in and out of consciousness.

Wilson said, "I think we should stay here until the Allies get here. What do you think, PFC Jeffery?"

"I think we should relocate away from this death pit. Let Johnny rest for the night and we'll try to move him to the medical building tomorrow. There's some comfortable-looking beds in there."

Wilson said, "I think we should make an effort to bury our dead."

Jeffery responds, "I don't necessarily agree with you. They wouldn't want to be buried here. They would want to be buried at their family cemetery. The Allies must be fairly close for the Nazis to clear out like they did."

"Well, it could be a day, or it could be a month. We need to at least separate them from the dead Nazi devils."

Jeffery responds, "We can do that tomorrow. Thirty-two dead and only four of us left. Man, that was quite an undertaking. We knew this morning that we would be up against it before they came for us. We were the lucky ones. Oh hell, I brought some food for you. I'm going to get Joe and the cook. What do you think?"

"I'll stay with Johnny. You all might as well stay in there where it's more comfortable."

"All right. By the way, those two guard dog beasts are out roaming around. I should've let Joe kill the black demons. Anyway, keep your eyes open tonight. They'll probably return to their home tonight."

"We'll do."

Jeffery went back to the main camp.

Joey and his mother became closer since they are by themselves, but he knew his mother yearned for Johnny every day. Joey attempted to emulate Johnny in every way. He had built himself into a smaller version of his older brother. No matter what he done, it was never enough to get the recognition Johnny received. He considered himself a failure. Right now, Johnny wasn't anyone to emulate as he hung on by the breath of his one good lung.

The sheriff believed Thomas Major was the killer of William, but he didn't have enough evidence to charge him. He hoped one day that the corpse of William would show up with the evidence to get Thomas behind bars. He told Joey and Lillian to tell him if they were bothered by the Majors. He asked about Johnny, but there wasn't anything new about him since his disappearance.

Corporal Wilson held Johnny to give him warmth and comfort. He knew about people clinging to life and the human touch. He had seen it in the war. Wilson took care of Johnny, but the blood and guts that took place today wouldn't allow him to rest. The continuous onslaught of machine gun bullets spraying the men and the buildings was a traumatic experience that he hoped would never transpire again in his life. As he smoked some cigarettes that he took off a dead Nazi, he heard growling of the two guard dogs that had lived in the confinement yard ever since he had been isolated there. They had returned like Jeremy said they probably would. Wilson didn't want them lurking around during the night. So, he opened fire on the two black devils.

He shot both with one instantly killed while the other ran off yelping.

Jeremy came back out to check on Wilson and Johnny. Jeremy said, "I see one of the bastards came back."

Wilson responded, "They both came back. The other one is probably off dying some place. I'd be cautious. Those two dogs were the most vicious I've ever seen."

"You better check that with Johnny. A dog or dogs really chewed him up."

"Yeah. They're man killers. I hope they took the rest of them on the train. They're more dangerous than a wolf."

"I always heard that most wolves are scared of man, but these bastards have been trained to attack man."

Wilson says, "Well, I've got plenty of bullets for them."

"I don't want to scare you, but if there's anymore, they could be hunting in packs."

"That'll make me feel good with all these dead men around me."

"I'll stay with you Corp. I ought to tell Joe about the change. I'll be back in a few minutes."

"Hold on Jeremy. What's the latest at the main camp?"

"We are sleeping on the hospital beds. Joe was teaching the cook how to speak English, but the cook wants to teach Joe how to speak German. Do you need some more water?"

"Yeah. You know we ought to have a watch in one of the guard posts."

"Can we wait until tomorrow?"

"Yeah. It's been more than enough that went on

today."

Jeremy returned and the night is quiet.

The next morning came and Jeremy woke up and said, "The boogey man didn't get us, but to wake up next to forty-three corpses is more than a man can take. We've got to get Johnny over to the hospital before it begins to smell awful ripe around here."

Wilson firmly said, "Thirty-two brave men died yesterday. We wouldn't be alive today if it wasn't for them."

"I know that Corporal Wilson and we'll take care of our own today. Maybe, a few words needs to be said over them."

Wilson agreed and asked Jeremy, "Is there a hospital bed with wheels over there?"

"Yeah. I'll wheel it over Corp. Is he still alive?"

"Yes, he's alive. I wouldn't be asking you if he wasn't."

Jeremy returns with the bed and they place Johnny on it. Wilson said after checking Johnny. "He's still alive. Let's roll it slow and easy. He needs new dressings when we get there."

After a very slow transport, they get him into the hospital unit.

For the first time, Wilson saw the inside of the Nazi camp building. He saw a swastika symbol on the wall and immediately yanked it down and stomped on it. Everyone looked at the furious corporal.

He asked angrily, "Why does everyone look surprised that I'm angry? To me, this damn symbol means only death and destruction. Remember how we got here and what happened to our comrades. I'll never forget this goddamn war."

They knew he was correct, but they can only look down and remain quiet at this time.

While Wilson made a walk-thru the building, Jeremy and Joe saw that Johnny's back was covered in blood, mostly dried, but some fresh. They went ahead and changed his dressings after cleaning him up.

Jeremy attempted talking to Johnny as he laid there with his eyes barely open. "Johnny, can you talk?"

Johnny slowly spoke, "I hear you."

"You survived that bloodbath. So, don't die on us, now. Do you understand?"

"Yeah."

Wilson returned from his trip through the building. "I see you got some new dressings on Johnny. Is he still bleeding out?"

"Yeah, he is Corporal. He can talk but not much."

"Put a blanket on him. It is kind of cold in here." Wilson looked at the cook and told him through sign language, "I want you to cook a soup with some stock in it for him. Do you understand?"

The cook nodded his head. Wilson said, "You better understand because I'm going to be watching you make it."

The cook made enough for them all to eat. Johnny sipped on the soup for the next few days and life began to show in him. His color returned and he began to talk more.

Wilson and the others smelled the dead bodies when the wind blew their way. Masked, they and the cook spread lime over each bunch of bodies.

After a week, they ran out of food. Joe, a lean, slow talking Kentuckian where hunting was a part of life. He killed a few game animals around the perimeters of the camp to keep the five of them alive.

One day while hunting, he heard tanks nearing the camp and he could only hope they were the Allied. He went to tell the others. They came out and listened for the approaching tanks with caution. Johnny could hear them while he lay on the hospital bed.

The four of them waved a white flag as the tanks rolled into the forsaken camp. Soon, they were met by American troops. It was a glorious day for the survivors of the camp.

Chapter Eleven
The Return

The American troops set up a temporary camp at the ex-Nazi Camp. In three days, the POWs, dead and alive, would be sent home. As the days ticked by, Johnny improved to where he could sit up and talk well. He began thinking about being home again, but first he would spend some recovery time in Walter Reed Hospital in Washington, D.C.

Johnny's mother was notified of his whereabouts and condition. They began writing to each other again. His mother didn't know what to write when he asked about his father. She told of his disappearance and how no one had come up with anything on him. Joey wrote and said he believed the Majors killed him. There was no doubt in Johnny's mind who did it.

Johnny had nightmares during his sixty day stay in recovery. The staff was aware of it as he screamed out a few times. They knew what he had went through and his dreams were just as horrifying. One nightmare, he attempted to escape the Nazis and Joey was with him, but he kept losing Joey and he would go back and try to find him and so the nightmare went on until he found Joey with his head cut off.

The doctor in charge transferred him to Major

General Hospital on Long Island, NY for psychiatric evaluation and treatment. He stayed there for a month and was treated with electric shock. He was sent home, with a bottle of pills, and his mother and Joey were waiting at the train station for him when he arrived.

They greeted him with open arms, but they knew he was not himself physically or mentally. He smiled and cried as he embraced both. He was thin and pale. They knew he had been a POW, but they didn't know the struggle his entailed. Joey drove the buggy home as they attempted to converse with the quiet Johnny. He had tried to talk with them as he did before, but he couldn't. Something had changed inside him.

Susan didn't meet him because she got married while Johnny was gone. Once back at home, Johnny began to help on the farm. He was slower but every bit as dependable. He and Joey rode their horses to town and Johnny bought enough whiskey to last him for a few days. Joey took a swig of it one day and spit it out.

Joey asked Johnny, "How do you drink that nasty tasting stuff?"

"It eases the pain."

"Are you talking about the wounds you got in the war?"

"Yeah, something like that."

It was Christmas 1945, and Johnny had been back a year. The war of all wars ended. They all decorate the tree together and it is an enjoyable time. Johnny had the whiskey bottle always nearby.

Johnny had stopped taking the pills and the nightmares returned. He was more sociable without the pills, but the nightmares scared everyone in the house. He didn't like himself anymore because he felt weak and no longer in control. He would break into cold sweats thinking about how he had been damaged by the Nazis. It had a hold of him and always would.

Joey started having trouble again with Quincy's boy, Tobie, and two of his friends. They had all outgrown the five-feet-seven-inch Joey by more than a few inches and they knew they had quite the advantage. Joey was a tough scrapper, but he knew he couldn't take on more than one. They shoved him after school, and he pushed their hands off him. When they continued to push him around, he realized he was going to get beaten up.

Suddenly, a truck drove up and Johnny stepped out of it. Although he physically is not what he was before the war, but the teenage boys do not know that. He had a jacket on that makes him look larger than he was.

When Joey yells, "Johnny."

He walks toward them with his scruffy beard and blood shot eyes. He looks madder than hell and they fear the legendary Johnny especially after him coming back as a war hero. Johnny said, "Don't let me see or hear about you all messing with Joey again. Do you hear me?"

The three startled young men realized this is not the time to mess with Joey and Johnny. They nodded their heads and slowly walked away.

Johnny and Joey got in the vehicle and drove away. Joey asked, "Where did you get the truck?"

"I bought it in town. They sold it to me at a low price since I got those medals in the war or that's what they say anyway. Looks like I showed up the right time. Doesn't it?"

"I'm glad you're back from that war. Now, you'll

really be here for me when I need you. How fast will the truck go?"

"I don't know yet. We'll try it out on the forestry road one day. Do you like it?"

"Yeah. I sure do. It's a ford. Ain't it?"

"Yep. No more of the bumpy wagon for us."

"You are the greatest, Johnny."

"Nahh. I'm just trying to help us along."

"You were sending your paycheck to mother and that helped us make it while you and father was gone. I hope some of you rubs off me, because I can't make myself be like you."

Johnny grinned and responded, "You don't need to be like me. You can take care of yourself and you're a good-looking young man. You will grow up to be a man that won't need me."

"You may be right and you may not."

Johnny chugged his whiskey bottle and threw it into the woods as they drove through the shady road. They went on to town and bought more whiskey.

That night, they built a large fire and looked at the stars. As a rarity, Lillian is with them.

She smiled as she commented, "So, this is what you two do when you are out to midnight."

Joey responded, "Johnny brought me out when I was a little boy and I would come out when he was gone and talk to him through the stars. Did you hear me, Johnny?"

"For a while I watched them, Joey, but things got bad over there… really bad."

Lillian stiffens as she heard Johnny say that. She had seen his body wounds and she knew his mind was not at a 100%.

Joey asked Johnny, "You said most of your scars are from dog bites, but there are other kinds of scars on you. What happened over there?"

Johnny looked down and looked into the stars. "It is too hard to explain. It's best that I leave it in the past."

Lillian responded, "Your condition tells me enough without going into detail."

It is quiet until Joey responded, "If it wasn't for your toughness, you wouldn't be here tonight."

"Perhaps not."

Lillian said, "I'm so happy you made it back home. I've missed you more than you can imagine."

It was quiet for a minute. Joey wanted to say something, but he wondered why his mother talked as if he wasn't even there.

Johnny responded, "When I was in that POW camp, I wanted to be back home more than you can imagine. I'm here now and I want to know what happened to Daddy. Has the sheriff said anymore about it?"

Lillian replied, "I haven't seen him to ask."

Johnny and Joey wasn't surprised at her answer since they knew she didn't love him anymore.

Johnny said, "Let's lay back and watch the stars."

Lillian wrapped her arm around Johnny and laid her head on his shoulder. Johnny and Joey felt bad for her obvious partiality. Joey had fell in love with his mother when Johnny was gone, but now it was hurting him more than ever. He didn't blame Johnny because he knew his mother was behind the hurt.

They watched the stars as Joey lay by himself until Johnny told him to come lie on the other side of him. He held onto Johnny as if he would never let go. Johnny knew he was dearly loved by both, but he wanted his mother to love Joey too. He could feel how Joey was starving for love by the pressure he was placing on Johnny's arm.

The cold months were closing fast. Johnny sat in the barn with a fire in a pit he dug. His mother wanted him to come in, but he and she knew he needed to be alone. His mind was clouded by his failures and future. He felt no one could help him out of his state of mind. He started taking his pills again to keep him from going crazy.

Joey was out of school for the summer. He and Johnny worked the gardens together and talked when Johnny wanted. The medicine made him have less energy and Joey increased his workload to pick up what Johnny lacked while Johnny drank whiskey outside the barn on a bench he constructed.

When Joey finished, he sat down by Johnny and asked, "Johnny, when do you think you'll be back to your old self?"

"I can't. I'm messed up, Joey."

"The war did this to you. Why did it make you messed up?"

"You can't understand unless you went through it. I did the best I could, but it wasn't good enough."

Joey asked, "Why did you get all those medals and they send you a check every month?"

"The medals are worthless, and the check is because I was wounded so badly that I can't work like normal people. The check is only good for folks that are poor like us."

"I don't understand."

"You may one of these days."

Joey is surprised to hear Johnny talk that way. He believed Johnny was drunk as he had been most of the time since he came back home.

As the summer heat pressed in over a hundred degrees, Johnny and Joey decided to ride down to the creek and cool off. There were a dozen people down there and Johnny didn't remove his cut-off sleeve shirt due to the appearance of the scars. There were still dog bite scars on his legs and arms. People stared at Johnny because they had never seen anything like the scars he had. The gargantuan black German Shepherds had ripped Johnny up so bad he would carry the scars forever.

Joey wasn't ashamed of his brother, but he worried that the Majors would find out that he wasn't in good condition. He knew Willard and C.R. had made it back from the war and they were in good condition. So, he stood in front of Johnny as much as he could.

Johnny dived into the creek and came up with an exhilaration holler. "That feels good, Joey. Dive in."

He does and they stand in chest deep water enjoying the cool creek water. Joey asked after pushing his wet hair back, "Why don't we do this more often?"

"We can, but you can take the truck down here when you want."

"I don't know how to drive."

"You'll start learning when we head back later."

"I don't want to wreck your new truck, Johnny."

"We'll manage."

"I'm surprised you're not drinking."

"It's best that I don't with all these people. None of

them are drinking. If they leave, I may pull it out."

Joey responded candidly, "I wish you would quit drinking for good."

"I can't do it. It helps me make it through the day. You know I rarely drank before the war. Now, I can't stop. Maybe one day, you'll know what I mean. I don't want you to drink and find out the hard way, but I would like for you to know that I need it to survive."

"I won't say anything else about it."

Suddenly, two young women come up to them and ask, "Are you Johnny Holland?"

"I am and this is my younger brother, Joey and who do we have the pleasure talking to?"

The smaller and prettier one responded, "I'm Shannon and this is my sister, Beverly. I went to school with you, but I was older than you. You probably don't remember me. I heard you were a war hero."

"I do remember you. Where is your man?"

"I don't have one. I got married, but it didn't work out. I got an annulment."

"Then, we need to reacquaint ourselves. How about me bringing out my bottle and celebrating this occasion."

Shannon said, "I don't drink, Johnny."

Johnny said in a low voice, "I guess we'll just talk about you."

She responded, "No. I want to talk about you. What did you do to become a war hero?"

Johnny looks down to the water and replied, "I don't consider myself a war hero."

She responded with a slightly louder voice, "Johnny, they don't give out medals to people that didn't do anything. You must've done something."

Joey was waiting for him to say something and when he didn't, he spoke up, "He did a lot over there." Joey knew Johnny didn't want to talk about it because he never really told him much."

"Thanks, Joey. I helped my company battle the Nazis in France before I was captured and I helped prevent some POWs, including myself, from being slaughtered. I was wounded multiple times during the time I was over there."

Shannon asked, "How did you prevent yawl from being killed?"

"By facing machine guns empty-handed."

Joey had never heard that before and was shocked to hear of something like that.

Shannon said somberly, "You deserve more than they gave you."

"Well, there were thirty-six of us and when the last Nazi was killed, there were only four of us that survived. Most of the thirty-six were as useful as me — enough of all that. Where do you and your sister live?"

"We live with our parents on Red Hill."

Johnny asked, "How did you get down here?"

"We rode with our neighbor." She points to the couple with three children.

"Do you want Joey and myself to take you both home?"

"I don't know. We need to talk about it."

Johnny doesn't pressure them because of his body maybe a turnoff with all his scars. His self-esteem drops lower than he would like. The communication slows down between them and the young women. When the family gets ready to depart, Shannon and Beverley went with them. Shannon does provide

Johnny an invitation to call on her.

After they depart, Johnny said, "I guess she didn't want to be with a war hero. Did she Joey?"

Joey replied, "It wasn't you. Beverley is in school with me and she's older and probably doesn't like me."

Johnny carefully responds, "I don't think they were ready for two studs like us."

Chapter Twelve
Back Home

They get ready to leave the creek and Johnny said, "I want you to drive us home."

"What do I do?"

"You've seen me do the same thing over and over. Joey cranked the vehicle and pressed on the clutch and placed the vehicle in first gear. He removed his foot off the clutch and the vehicle dies.

Johnny said, "This time leave the foot on the clutch and press the gas pedal a little before taking your foot off the clutch. That will get you going and then shift into second. Switch gears from first to second without pressing on the gas pedal. This way you'll know how to switch gears when I tell you. Go ahead and try again."

Joey was successful in getting the truck going and Johnny instructed him through the gear shifting. Joey does good until a vehicle came toward him on the dirt road. Joey swerved away from the vehicle and Johnny grabbed the steering wheel, but it was too late because Joey sideswiped a tree. He kept driving as Johnny sipped on his bottle.

They arrive home and looked at the damaged right side of the vehicle. Joey puts his hands behind his head and said, "I'm sorry for wrecking your truck, Johnny. I was afraid that I would do something stupid like that."

"Don't worry about it, Joey. I told you to drive."

After they ate that evening, Johnny and Joey go laid out under the stars on this sweltering hot night. The locusts was buzzing all around them, but so were swarms of mosquitos which seemed to be out on windless nights like this one. They had put on some mosquito repellant that helped from being bitten so much.

Joey said after looking at the moon, "Mrs. Gray said that those dark spots on the moon are craters caused by meteorites hitting the moon. What do you think?"

"She's probably right. The moon is older than the Earth and that is why there is more craters on the moon than Earth."

"I think the Earth is older than the Moon because the Earth is a lot bigger."

"That has nothing to do with it. In fact, you probably are making my case for me because the Moon has been beaten down over the years while the Earth is younger and full of life. The Moon is dead. There may be some natural resources in the Moon, but I don't think any life is on the Moon."

Joey thought about what Johnny said and responded, "What about space monsters?"

"I don't think there's anything on the surface of the moon but some desolate land."

"I'll have to ask Mrs. Gray about that."

"Don't ask her anything like that because she doesn't know."

"Probably not."

It becomes quiet for a spell. Joey asked, "Why did

you tell those girls about what happened in the war and never told me?"

"I didn't know if you were ready to hear about that and when they kept asking, I decided to at least give a little about my experience in the war. Believe me, there is so much more, but I believe it's best to leave that over there and try not to think about it over here."

"I guess you're right."

When school started back, Johnny asked Joey, "How's school going for you?"

"It's going okay. You know."

"Are you getting passing grades?"

"Most of the time."

"Why not all the time?"

"There's too much to learn and a lot of it is boring."

"What's boring?"

"Math and English."

"You'll need to learn those subjects as you get older. I had to use them in the Army, and we need to keep count of things here on the farm. Our mother uses math for cooking."

"I know how to add and subtract, but I don't know how to do fractions."

"How are you and Mrs. Gray getting along?"

"Okay."

"I'll help you learn fractions and whatever else you need help with. Bring the problems home with you and Mrs. Gray will have a new respect for you in a few days."

A few days later, Joey came home and told Johnny that he got an 'A' on his math test.

Johnny said with a big smile. "Let's celebrate by going to the creek and you drive while I drink from my party bottle."

Joey responded with a joyful, "Yes."

They made it to the creek when it was late afternoon and there's no one there. Joey said, "We got it to ourselves."

"I figured we would. I came down here, about this time of year, while you were in school before I went in the Army and it was like this. This is a good time to come because the days are still warm and there's rarely any people down here. The water is slightly cooler because of the shorter days. You can feel fall in the air."

"You make me excited with what you just said. You got something about you that makes people listen. You don't waste words."

"Thank you, Joey. I appreciate that. Let's get in the water before the sun starts going down."

They dived in the water and Johnny starts a water wrestling match. It doesn't take long before he ducks Joey underwater.

Joey said, "I'll probably never be able to beat you in wrestling or anything else."

"Sure, you will. I am an old man way before my time."

"I don't know about that. You've lived through more than any man can."

"I'm not so sure about that, but anyway, I am a much older man because of what I have survived through. Do you understand?"

"I think I do. We'll you ever get better again?"

"I'll never get back to what I once was, but I could get better than I am. Tell me how you aced your test."

Joey replied, "I just followed what you taught me, and I took one problem at a time."

"I'm so happy that I could help you. The sun is going down. Enjoy the water the next few minutes and we'll head home."

They take a dive and walk back to the truck.

Johnny was buying liquor at a store where an attractive woman worked. Each time he went, they talked a little more until she asked him over. She was a thirty-nine-year old divorcee with a mysterious past. She had dark hair, black eyes, and an attractive face with a small to medium size figure. She was as much intrigued about Johnny as he was her. She could have asked probably any man to come over and they would've come over, but Johnny was somewhat of a legend around these parts and she wanted to see what kind of man he really was.

He came over to her room in the town hotel. She had a room in the old white painted three-story building. She had to share a bathroom with the other third floor occupants. It was a typical small-town hotel of the time. She had fried some chicken and potatoes with ice-tea. Dessert was some small fried peach pies.

After eating, Johnny compliments her food she cooked, "Doris, that was as tasty as my mother's cooking and she cooks really good."

"I'm glad you liked it, Johnny. I learned to cook from my mother."

"Where is your mother and family?"

"In Arkansas as far as I know."

"That's not too far away. You don't see them often. Do you?"

"No. It's been a number of years."

"Why?"

"There's too little I want to remember from back there. Enough about me. How does it feel being a war hero?"

"I don't consider myself a hero. I just happened to be the one that survived with all the wounds."

"I think you were a hero because you are also thought of highly by most people around here that doesn't even mention you with the war. The Majors are the exception. I think they are jealous of your reputation."

"I wish you wouldn't even have mentioned that bunch. I've had to fight them most of my life."

"Well I won't mention them anymore if you'll come a little closer." Both leaned into each other until they kissed. Johnny turned the light off. It is only a minute before they both are nude and all over each other.

After the sex, Doris asked Johnny, "You must like the light off when you get it on."

"I don't want you to get turned off to my wounds all over my body."

"You wear long sleeve shirts and the only scar I ever seen is on your left hand. It looks like a bite by an animal."

"Well, my whole body is covered with them plus some shrapnel and bullet wounds."

"I could feel some on your back."

He stayed all night and part of the morning with her before she goes to work at noon. She cooked them breakfast before she started getting ready. Johnny said he would see her later at the store and went on home.

Once at home, Joey and Lillian was worried

about him. Johnny said with a slight grin, "I told yawl I had a date last night."

Lillian said sarcastically, "That was last night. It's nearly noon the next day. I just worry about you. I don't want you to not come back like your father did."

"Well, I'll try to give you a heads-up next time about being late coming home."

Joey asked, "Are we going hunting this afternoon?"

"Sure, we are. How about four?"

"Sure."

"That'll give me time to take a nap."

Lillian said cynically, "It sounds like you didn't get much sleep last night."

Johnny lay in bed thinking about Doris instead of sleeping. She knew how to treat a man. He had never met anyone like her. He wanted her as his own woman. He fell asleep at that thought.

Johnny awakened as Joey come to check on him. They went hunting, but Johnny had Doris on his mind. In fact, it was the first time, Joey ever killed more squirrels than his brother. Joey knew something was different about Johnny. He looked as if he was watching something in the distance and he wasn't as talkative. He was blind with love.

That night, Joey asked Johnny if he would watch the stars with him and he did.

As they laid on the ground with a perfect night, Joey asked the quiet Johnny, "I hope you never forget me."

"That's ridiculous. I love you more than I do my own mother."

"Why would you love me more than her?"

"I felt you needed love more than her and daddy. They didn't show you love like they should have. I raised you until that damn war. I worried about you while I was gone, and I've tried to make up for it since I've been back. I thought you knew that."

"I do, but I don't want it to end. What if you leave here?"

"I'm not going anywhere. Where would I go?"

"You could change your mind."

"We can't worry about what may happen in the future. There's only so much you can control and after that, fate will take its course."

The inquiring Joey asked, "What does fate mean?"

"It means the way each one of our lives was meant to turn out."

"Who makes our fate turn out?"

"Our parents, education, people in our life, and experiences. Once you have lived your life to a certain point, your fate will be revealed if you care to believe it."

Chapter Thirteen
Another War

It was Sunday and Johnny knew Doris would be off work today. He went over before lunch—hoping to take her out to eat.

She slightly opened door when he knocked. She said, "You're up early moving around. Come in Johnny. Would you like some coffee?"

"I guess I'll take a cup. I've already drank three cups at the house."

"That's nothing for me since I drink it all day long."

"Yeah. I do notice you have a cup nearby you at the store all the time."

She poured them a cup and tells him to sit down at the table. "What's on your mind this morning Mr. Holland?"

"I want to take you to lunch wherever you like."

He looked at her while she took a draw on a cigarette and exhaled. She looked at him as she tapped the ashes into the ashtray.   "You want to go out and fight the church crowd at lunch?"

"Well, isn't there somewhere to go where they're not around."

"Not really." She grinned. "Why don't you take

me out to dinner Thursday evening?"

"Yeah, but I want to see you before then."

"You got a spot in my bed whenever you want, Johnny." She provides him — 'I want you stare.'

They spend the day together in bed and played themselves into a state of hunger. "Our stomachs are growling, Johnny. How about if I fix us some eggs and sausage?"

"That sounds like a good idea."

She slipped into a sheer nightgown as she asked him, "How do you like your eggs?"

"Over medium—like you."

"Are you comparing me to an egg?"

"Yep. You got a medium build and you look good all over."

"I never heard that one before."

"I guess you've heard a lot of lines?"

"I've heard plenty."

Johnny dressed and sat at the table—watching his gem of a woman preparing his food. He watches how she moves and looks at him. He can see her sexy body through the negligee.

She said by looking out the corner of her eye, "Are you going to let me finish cooking?"

"Sure. I'm starving."

"I wonder—you're getting me upset watching me so quiet like."

"I'm sorry. I'm just admiring you."

She placed the plates with eggs, sausage, and toast on the table. She handed him the utensils and coffee before sitting down with him. They eat quietly until Johnny finishes his food.

He complimented her cooking before sipping

on his coffee.

She stopped eating and takes another drink of coffee. "I'm glad you liked it."

"You cooked them like a real pro."

"I've had plenty of practice. I was a cook at a diner a few years ago."

"I'm surprised you aren't married."

"I gave that up years ago."

"Don't you get lonely living by yourself?"

"Sometimes. I've met a new friend in you. You are quite a talker once you feel comfortable around someone. I like your style, Johnny. You're a good man."

Johnny stayed another night with her.

He came home and Joey was in school. Lillian said to him, "Your dates are becoming long and longer. Joey was worried about you when he left for school this morning and I was too. I thought you were going to let me know when you were going to stay over."

She gave him a stern look expecting a reasonable answer. "I'm sorry that I didn't think ahead. Don't worry about me staying overnight when I go over there."

She responded, "You said she worked at that store on the edge of town. I haven't seen any young women working in there. Wait a minute, are you seeing the woman in there that's my age?"

He was hesitant to answer, but he does. "That's right. That's who I've been seeing."

"Why don't you find someone closer to your age. There's no telling how many men that woman has went through. Did you ever think about that?"

"I kind of have. You don't know anything about her to be saying things like that."

"Neither do you. Johnny, you need to think this through. You've always been smart."

Angrily, he asked, "Did you think it through what you did to Joey's life?"

On the edge of tears, she asked, "What are you saying?"

"You know what I'm saying. I thought about it enough to know Joey wasn't Daddy's child."

She starts crying loudly. "Oh, Johnny—Why did you have to say that to me? I made a stupid mistake and I've paid for it."

"What about poor Joey? He's been paying for it his entire life? Who is his real father?"

"Stop it! Just stop it — please."

He stepped out on the porch and sat in a chair to clear his head. He can hear her crying from inside the house. He felt bad for hurting his mother, but he knew Joey is the innocent one that has paid for her sins. He decided to go dig potatoes to keep his mind stable. He can't allow himself to fall into another depression.

While he dug potatoes, his mind was cluttered with thoughts about Doris, Mother, Joey, and his father. After digging all the potatoes, he washes up and drives to the store to see Doris.

When he entered the store, he saw Doris talking to a man at least her age. He was a slender man, dark hair and blue eyes, slightly shorter than Johnny. They were smiling and laughing. She had her eyes on Johnny as soon as he entered the store. She didn't stop talking to the man and she didn't take her eyes off Johnny as he approached them.

When he got in front of them, she spoke to him, "Hello, Johnny. Johnny, this is Angel and Angel, this is the war hero Johnny Holland. I'm sure you read about him in the town newspaper."

Johnny looks the man straight in the eye and the man looks at Johnny in his short sleeve shirt. "Johnny, I thought you were fighting Germans. From the look of it, you were fighting bears."

"I don't find that comical at all."

Doris attempted to halt any friction, "Angel, Johnny is sensitive about his war scars. Johnny, he didn't many any harm."

Johnny responded firmly, "I find it disrespectful."

"I didn't mean anything except you must be as tough as your reputation."

Johnny responded demandingly, "I believe it's time for you to leave."

"I'll go this time but be careful how you talk to me. I can be just as rough as you."

"You want to prove it?"

"Not today. Cool down, Johnny. I'll see you later, Doris."

She responded, "Okay, Angel."

He walked out of the store and Johnny asked, "Is that your man on the side?"

"He's just a friend. Are you jealous?"

"Should I be?"

"No."

"You two seemed awful chummy."

"Johnny, I like you a lot, but don't ruin it."

He doesn't have anything else to say except, "Give me a fifth of Jim Bean and I'll be on my way."

She sold him his bottle as she stared at him until he

walked out the door.

While he drove home, he took a swig from his bottle and began to think about Doris and Angel and what if they were just friends and not lovers. With that thought, he contemplated to still seeing her, but he remembered what is mother said about her. His mind went back and forth until he arrived home. He went out to the barn and drank on his bottle.

A mid-fall cool front was pushed through the area. There was some rain as it pushed through. He watched the rain drip off the tin roof while he sat on a bale of hay with the bottle in his hand. The barn blocked off most of the wind, which made it somewhat comfortable after the warm morning. He was at peace for the moment, but there were plenty of things to worry about and he felt that he should get back on the medicine in case he falls off into a depression. He still had nightmares of the war but hid them as much as possible.

When Joey came home from school, Johnny told him that he would no longer have to worry about riding the horse to school. "Joey, I've decided that I will bring you to school and bring you home from school from now on."

"Are you sure, Johnny? I know you sleep late sometimes, and you weren't here this morning."

"I'm sure. We'll start in the morning. You are my priority from now on."

"I thought I was anyway until you met that gal."

"There's no gal ahead of you and there never will be. Remember that."

Johnny and his mother are quiet at supper. Joey sensed the tension between them. Lillian is more attentive to Joey than normal and Johnny and Joey both like her new approach to him.

As the year went on, Johnny held to his promise to Joey. He did see Doris occasionally until he found out her and Angel were seeing each other more than he could stand. He told his mother she was right about Doris.

She said lovingly, "I was only looking out for you. You know I love you more than anything in this world."

Johnny likes that she loves him so much, but Joey is never mentioned and that bothers him about her.

As the years go by, Joey gets to a point in school that he knows he will not graduate, and he quits school. Johnny attempted to help him, but Joey had given up. He had lost complete interest and Johnny knew it.

The year was 1950 and the United Nations, primarily the United States, had entered war in Korea because of communist China and communist Soviet Union backing Northern Korea to expand into Southern Korea. Johnny knew that Joey would be called to serve in the military if the conflict continued.

In 1951, the draft notice came, and Joey passed the entrance exam. He was to report to Fort Hood.

Johnny told him afterwards, "You should have intentionally failed the exam with you being a high school drop-out. It would have worked out to your advantage."

"It's too late for that, Johnny. I hope that I don't come back like you did. I need to prove to myself and everyone else that I can do this."

Johnny and his mother took Joey to the bus station and sent him off with love and hope. Johnny is sickened about Joey going into a war that could possibly turn out bad.

Joey and Johnny wrote each other nearly every day while he was in recruit training. Even his mother wrote him a couple of letters with Johnny's urging. His training went smoother than Johnny's did, but he was assigned to the 23rd Infantry Regiment and didn't get any leave or extra training. He went straight to South Korea and was assigned to a squad that was preparing to take a ridge at the front.

It was September 13th, 1951 and Joey was entering a nightmare. He watched for hours the bombardment of the ridge by American aircraft, tanks and artillery. The barren hillside became a cratered hill.

Without any pep talks, Joey and his platoon was ordered to take the hill. Joey just did whatever one else begun doing in his squad which was scampering up the hill and looking for cover as they ascended the ridge. He watched the leaders take out one enemy bunker after another. The American casualties began to mount as they neared the top. Joey didn't know if he had killed any of the enemy, but he had shot most of his M1 rifle ammunition. A counterattack came with surges of fresh North Koreans unwavering attempt to retake the relocations they lost. The battle became even closer as the fighting became hand to hand combat. Joey was attacked by more than a few of the enemy. He still had his grenades and some rifle ammunition. He used that to work his way back down the ridge. Finding guns and ammunition from dead soldiers kept Joey at a point near the top. His hunting skills from back home assisted him in his survival on the ridge. Eventually, another platoon came up the ridge because his platoon had been severely decimated, and he no longer saw anyone he had seen before. He was exhausted and hungry with little ammo.

As he worked his way down the ridge, the men going up would ask him how bad it got. He would always say "Bad, really bad."

When he arrived at the base of the ridge, the 2nd Lieutenant in charge of his platoon said in astonishment, "Get this soldier a hot meal and a couple of days of rest. He's been up there since noon yesterday."

Joey ate and rested for two days. During this time, he thought about Johnny when he was a POW and suffered all his wounds mentally and physically. He had decided that he would not allow himself to be taken prisoner. He would go down fighting to his death.

A squad leader came to him and told him that he would be up next to accompany them up the ridge. Joey realized this was a suicide mission because the endless supply of Chinese was sending in troops to defend the ridge.

For the next two weeks, Joey killed several North Korean and Chinese soldiers. He made the climb up to the top a few more times. He would always place himself behind the first wave up the ridge to lessen his chances of being shot down, but his luck was about to run out as a new wave of North Koreans set up a machine gun to cover their forces descending the ridge toward the few Americans and French that had survived the ascent. Joey had become a pro at climbing up and down the mountain and he knew all the enemy's bunkers and hiding spots. Hunkered down in a pitted area, he shot the enemy coming toward him as if they were a shooting gallery. Knowing that his rifle could jam or run out of ammo while the enemy swarmed his position, he had no time to pay attention to anything, but what was in front of him.

Suddenly, he was under heavy machine gun fire from the top of the ridge. He had drawn their fire because of him shooting so many of their comrades. He could do nothing but hope they would fire somewhere else. Reloading his gun while bullets showered the ground all around him, an exposed area of his chest took a bullet that went straight through him. His body rolled over as bullets continued pelting around his body until they targeted someone else.

Everything went black as Joey laid there helpless. He regained consciousness an hour later as another wave ascended the ridge and found him still alive. He heard their voices calling for a medic.

As they took him down the ridge, he could hear gunfire like he had never heard before. Everything went black and when he awoke, he could hear the vibration of the helicopter. He lost consciousness again and awakened in a Mobile Army Surgical Hospital (MASH unit). They had done all they could considering his wound and were attempting to inform him of being transferred to an established hospital. He nodded his head and began a long recovery from one hospital to Walter Reed Hospital. There he made a full recovery in three months.

Johnny had received telegrams about his little brother's health progression, but he was having his own problems with severe depression. The pills were no longer effective, and the subtle Veterans Administration referred him to the VA Hospital in Houston, Texas. He needed the treatment, but he expected Joey to come home in a couple of days and he had no intention of being gone when he arrived.

Joey arrived in Woodville by train as expected while Johnny and his mother was waiting for him. He looked well despite his dreadful wound. They embraced one another and loaded up in the truck.

"You look good, Joey. How do you feel?" Johnny asked.

"Like a nightmare that has turned into a dream. I'm home, away from all that military stuff."

"Are you having any nightmares and depression?"

"I have nightmares after climbing that ridge so many times. There were thousands of men killed there. The nightmares are all about the same thing with only a few details being different."

Johnny worried about the aftermath of Joey's traumatic experiences. It was different than his, but in a way, just as disturbing.

It was a quiet drive home. Their mother cooked a deer roast, mashed potatoes and gravy, okra and tomatoes, and cornbread.

After the filling meal, Lillian asked her boys, "Would yawl like to go out to look at the starry sky with me?"

Both looked at each other as if 'when did Mother care about looking at the night sky?'

Both agreed to go with her. They put on their coats and Lillian brought out three blankets so they would each have one. The night was cool since it was nearing Christmas.

Lillian said, "I think we ought to celebrate Christmas this time. We've got a lot to be thankful for." She knew Johnny had been suffering from post-traumatic war problems but hoped this may help him with Joey at home.

Joey agreed and Johnny nodded his head. Joey asked, "Johnny, you've been quiet since I've been in. Is there anything I can do?"

Johnny shook his head. "I've missed you." He starts crying and his mother moved over next to him and embraced him. Joey does the same.

Joey said kindly, "Don't worry, Johnny, I'll get a job and won't be a burden on you and Mother. I'll help around the place like I always did before."

Johnny shook his head while still sobbing, "It's not you, it's me. I can't forget the horrors I went through. I don't want you to go through what I've had to."

"I realize that. I just don't want you to get in over your head with everything."

Lillian spoke up, "He hasn't been well since you left. The VA wants him to check in the VA hospital in Houston."

Joey responded, "I'm back now and hopefully things will get better for all of us."

Johnny nodded his head and laid down on his back to clear his thoughts. "Remember, Joey, the very first time we watched the stars."

"I remember, Johnny. Even when I was amongst all that hell over there, I looked at the moon and stars and wished you would come help me out, but I knew you had your own demons to battle. I didn't think I would come back alive."

Johnny responded with hope, "You came back, and I love you even more. Always, keep that in mind."

"I won't forget it. Will you always be with me like you've been before?"

"I will."

Chapter Fourteen

Johnny's War

Joey cut a small pine tree and they all decorated it with pinecones, holly branches with berries, and white oak acorns on a twig of the white oak tree that he gathered. Johnny always had his bottle close to him which made him more sociable at such a happy time. Lillian and Joey had a shot of Johnny's rum in their eggnog to add to the joy of their togetherness at this time. It was a joyous occasion that had been lacking since they were a family again.

As the new year of 1953 started, Joey begun making his rounds hunting a job. He found his service in the Korean War to be useless in the small town full of nepotism and favoritism. He would feel disappointed coming home and being asked if he had any luck. Finally, they had quit asking. He knew that he had no chance of improving himself while he remained there.

Johnny seemed to feed off Joey's frustration which sent him tumbling back into a serious depression. He stayed in his room for nearly two weeks. Joey attempted to talk to him, but he wouldn't say much back.

Joey and his mother talked about getting Johnny to the hospital in Houston. Joey asked Johnny, "Don't you think it would be better if you went to that hospital and see if they can help you out?"

Johnny sat up on the edge of the bed with his head down. He was silent for about a minute and said, "Yeah. I better go."

Joey and his mother took Johnny to Houston in Johnny's truck. They stayed all day waiting for a prognosis and at the end of the day, they were informed that he should stay a while for treatment. They said their goodbyes to Johnny and left.

On their long silent drive back home, his mother said, "I sure hope he'll be treated good there. I heard about places like that when I was young."

Joey asked, "What do you mean?"

"They put people in straight jackets where they can't move and keep you full of medicine that makes you so drowsy where you can't sit up. So, they tie you to chairs where you won't fall out."

"Johnny was in one in New York. He never said anything like that to me."

"He was too ashamed to say anything to us."

Joey became even more worried about his big brother. He would be sure to ask Johnny about the details of his treatment.

Joey took care of everything around the farm like Johnny did for so long. Joey had learned almost everything he knew from Johnny. He began to realize he would have to be the man of the house until Johnny got better.

For the next few months, they never heard from Johnny despite both writing to him. Joey wanted to work some outside of the farm. His mother advised him to go see some of William's employers and find out if they needed some work to be done.

He was given a chance by some of them, but he lacked the skills William had because he was never taught anything by him. He cleared fence lines, cut up firewood, and milked cows. Unable to do any type of construction, prevented him from making more than a few dollars a day. He took what he could get and felt he was doing the best he could.

He had nightmares quite often of him on that ridge but seemed to function during the day well enough. But he knew Johnny's problems was preventing Johnny from living anything close to a normal life.

Joey and his mother rarely talked. Joey had accepted his relationship with his mother, but he was lonely. He was not respected by anybody. The people he worked for talked condescendingly down to him. He needed a healthy Johnny back to provide him with some companionship.

Joey and his mother decided to drive into Houston to see what has happened to Johnny. When they arrive, they wait a couple of hours before anyone will come out to talk to them and when they do, they inform them that Johnny needs more treatment.

Joey is mad and said, "You've had him for five months and still needs more treatment. What kind of treatment are you doing to him?"

The doctor replied with rigidity, "We are providing him with the most modern procedures in the medical field of psychiatry. He is in poor condition mentally."

Joey said angrily, "This is his mother and I'm his brother and we want him out of here."

The doctor said with firmness, "If you insist on removing him from our care, you will have to sign documents for his release, and you will be responsible for him."

Joey responded emphatically, "Where's the documents? We'll both sign them."

"We will prepare him for release, but you're going

against my recommendation."

"We'll be waiting for him. How long will it take?"

"A few hours." The doctor replied and walked away to the mental health ward.

Joey and his mother go back to the truck to eat a sandwich. Joey said, "I don't like that doctor's fancy talk. It's nothing, but a coverup of what they're doing here."

Lillian said, "I just hope he's better."

"We've got to do whatever we can to make him happy. It's up to us to get him well. We can't count on those quacks anymore."

They walked back into the hospital and waited until Johnny is released to them. They embraced him and told him how much they loved him. He was glad to see them and informed them that he was thankful for them having him released.

On their way home, Joey and his mother attempted to converse with Johnny, but he would only answer the questions they asked. They didn't pry into any details, yet. His answers revealed enough for them to realize there was much more to his confinement.

Johnny took to the bottle as soon as he got situated at home. Joey drove him wherever he wanted to go. Johnny started opening-up to him when he started to get drunk.

Johnny said openly, "Them sorry motherfuckers was trying to break me with electroshock, Joey. They put me through that torture over a hundred times. I gritted my teeth and took whatever they tried on me. It drained me each time they did it, but I recovered knowing that they were doing me more harm than good."

"Why didn't you write us back when we wrote to you?"

"I saw the envelops that you all sent, but they kept me so sedated that I didn't know how to open them, and they disappeared before long. It was hell, Joey, I'm so happy that yawl got me out of that hell hole."

"I had a feeling that was what you were going through. After a while, I knew we had to do something."

"I'm glad you did. I would still be there if you hadn't."

"I know."

Joey and Johnny did everything together and Johnny's condition improved. He still drank as much as ever, but it helped him through every day. He was smoking a pack of cigarettes each day, which seemed to keep him calm.

Joey met a young woman, Elizabeth, at the creek one day and so his first love started. She was a redhead with a medium build and nineteen years old. He fell head over heels for her and started seeing her as much she could stand. Johnny warned him about a whirlwind romance, but he had never felt like this before.

Johnny accepted his time away from Joey, but he began to backslide into that deep depression again. His mother was always attempting to talk to him, but he didn't have much to say to her. She brought his food to the room and sometimes he would eat it and other times, it would sit there until she took it away. When Joey was around, he talked to him depending on how much he drank.

Joey asked him, "Is my time away from you causing

your depression to get worse?"

"I don't think so. Joey, I'm in bad shape. I don't know what to do."

"Is there anything I can do for you?"

"I wish I knew."

For the next few months, Joey continued to see Liz quite often, but he always tried to assist Johnny anyway he could. They sat out and watched the night sky every few evenings.

"Joey, you remember when I told you about the electroshocks?"

"Yes, I remember."

"They also put me in ice baths, and I heard them talking about doing a lobotomy on me. I don't want to go back there."

"What is a lobotomy?"

"I didn't know myself until I asked another patient. He told me, they cut the head open to get to the brain and cut on it while you're awake."

"I'm glad that we got there before they did that to you. They tortured you instead of helping you."

During the silence, Joey contemplated Johnny's experiences in and out of the hospital and decided it was necessary to discuss his time in war.

"Johnny, tell me what happened to you in the war."

Johnny opened up and told him of his horrifying experiences in the war and his captivity."

The roles of Johnny and Joey seemed to take a complete reversal with Joey now the anchor and Johnny the one needing help. "You are a warrior, Johnny. Somehow, we have to let the warrior go and let you live your life in peace."

"How?"

"Try to block those bad experiences out of your mind when they come on me. Think about now and maybe even the future when the nightmares come. It helps me out."

"Joey, I will try it. That's better advice than I have heard from any of the doctors I've talked to."

Johnny did get better, but he realized that he will never shake his dreadful past.

One evening Johnny wants Joey to take him to a local tavern. Joey is hesitant, but he takes him and goes in with him.

Johnny said with gusto, "The drinks are on me, Joey."

"You know I don't drink."

"Then, order a soda water and I'll pretend you're drinking with me."

"Okay."

The more Johnny drank, the more sociable he became. He went over to talk with two women at the bar. Joey watched him to ensure he did not make a fool of himself. The second hour past and Johnny would take turns dancing with each of the women. Joey sat alone watching his brother have a good time. He would motion for Joey to come join them, but he would not go because he would feel like he was cheating on Liz.

Finally, Johnny came over to Joey and asked him, "Why are you just sitting here? Why don't you come join us?"

"I wouldn't feel right about Liz. You know what I mean?"

"Yeah. I know what you mean. You're in love with

the only girl you've ever been with."

"How am I supposed to feel?"

Johnny smiled and answered through experience. "You'll come out of it in time. Look, if you get tired of sitting around, go on home. I'll get these girls to take me home when the night is over."

"I'm not leaving you here. I may go out to the truck and wait for you, but I'm not leaving without you. Do you understand?"

He answers with pacification, "Sure. I'm going back to my women. Come join us if you change your mind."

He went back to the women as Joey watched him buy all their drinks. Joey viewed the scene until 11PM. With the juke box blaring, he exited the tavern and sat in the truck observing the door until Johnny came out.

Chapter Fifteen

Time Stops

Joey began to doze off as he continued to wait for Johnny.

Inside the tavern, Johnny drank himself to drunkenness and now some of the Majors have entered the tavern. He sees C.R. and Quincy but ignores their presence as they order up at the bar. His mind became tangled thinking about them and his father's disappearance. Suddenly, the bartender brings Johnny another drink that was sent to him paid by the Majors. He glances over to them and they hold their drinks up to him. He knows he is drunk, and they know it too. He drank it and continues to ignore them while his mind becomes desperate for peace, but there cannot be peace with the Majors around.

The two women realized he's drunk and can see he is nonresponsive. They drift off without him realizing it. The Majors send him another drink, but he refuses it and attempts to depart the tavern because he doesn't know what to do.

The Majors intercepted him, and Quincy grabbed him by the arm and said, "Hold on Johnny. We'll take care of you."

They guided him back to the bar and he is so drunk, he does not attempt to stop them. They drank until Johnny could not stand up anymore. Each one of the Majors grabbed an arm of Johnny and basically dragged him outside.

With dreary Joey sitting behind the wheel of the truck, he looked up and thought he saw Johnny taken out of the tavern. Joey got out of the truck and sees the Major's truck drive off. He ran into the bar as the patrons were leaving at closing time. With no sign of Johnny, he ran back outside and got in the truck and floorboarded the truck in the direction the Majors went. He saw the taillights of a vehicle about a mile away before it disappeared over a hill. Driving the truck as fast as it would go and soon reached the top of the hill, he doesn't see the taillights because of the winding road, but he continues driving and thinking where they could be taking Johnny. He knew they are up to no good because they are going in the opposite direction of Johnny's home. Not thinking they are being followed, Joey thinks he has a chance of finding them. Desperation begins to set in after he passes some side roads. Not familiar with the roads and does not know where they end up. He continued to drive fast for a few miles, but thinking he should have caught them by now, he turned around and started taking the side roads for miles. He began to doubt if that was their vehicle. They could have taken a side road in town.

Joey continued searching until the truck is almost of out fuel. Parked at a gas station, he waited until it opened in the morning. As the sun began to rise, he is depressed and tired. He began to cry as he had failed in his attempt to find Johnny — afraid that Johnny would end up like his father.

Joey filled the truck up and drove to the Sheriff's Gentry's office. Walking into the office the sheriff asked, "What can I do for you young Holland?"

"I've got a missing person report to file on my brother."

The sheriff gave a serious look at Joey. "When did you last see him?"

"Last night at the tavern on the edge of town."

"He may show up today. Give him time to get home. What happened at that joint?"

Joey informed him of what happened last night.

The sheriff responded, "I'll drive out to your place to see if he showed up. If he isn't there, I'll be making a trip out to the Majors. I'll be out to your place not long after you get there."

The sheriff brought along his deputy and when they arrived, Lillian was sobbing her heart out after Joey informed her of the events that occurred. The sheriff can see that Johnny hasn't returned. He told Lillian and Joey that he will find Johnny if it's the last the thing he does. Joey says, "I'm sure Quincy was one of them because he was holding Johnny and he was a lot bigger than anyone else."

While the sheriff drove over to the Majors, he has a strong feeling that they were responsible for Johnny's vanishing.

When he arrived at the Majors' place, old man Major is sitting on the porch by himself.

He asked, "What brings you here this morning?"

"I need to know where you and your boys were last night?"

"Well sheriff, I was here last night, and my boys were probably at home with their families. My wife can tell you I was here all night."

The sheriff said, "I'll be back when I do some more checking."

The sheriff drove to the tavern and talked to the owner. He claimed he saw nothing, but the sheriff wanted to talk to the employees that were working last night. He found where they lived and went to talk with the barkeeper first.

A tall thin man opened the door after the sheriff knocked on it. "Hello, Slim. I'd like to talk with you about last night."

"What did I do wrong. I didn't sell to any minors."

"I'm not here about anything you done. I want to know if you saw Johnny Holland last night at the tavern."

"I did."

"Who was he with?"

"I'm not sure about that, but he was buying drinks for himself and two bar flies who come to the tavern a couple of nights a week."

"Who else was with him later that night?"

"Two of the Majors, Quincy and C.R. were buying him drinks. Johnny was drunk, drunk."

"Why was you selling him more drinks with him being so drunk?"

"The Majors were paying and I'm there to sell to

them."

"You know the history behind the Majors and the Hollands."

"I've heard some things like that, but I figured they made up because Johnny was drinking with them. You know, I've seen some strange things working at the tavern. People get in hellacious fights and the next night their best friends. Why are you asking me all this?"

The sheriff takes his hat off and wipes his brow and replied, "Johnny is missing, and his family is obviously worried about him."

"Well, Sheriff, Johnny maybe sleeping off that drunk somewhere. It's a little early for you to be jumping to conclusions since it's been less than twelve hours ago."

"It may sound to you that I'm jumping the gun, but his father disappeared something like this ten years ago. I'm not going to cold trail this disappearance like that one. The Majors were the main suspects in that one too."

"Well, Sheriff, I don't remember any of them being charged with anything."

"Look, I know the Majors are some of your regular customers, but I want your cooperation and you can start by sitting down right now and writing everyone's name in that tavern at closing time. You know who was there because most of them come there a lot."

After the sheriff got the names, he drove out to Quincy's place. He walks to the front screen door and his deputy walks to the back of the house.

Quincy's wife comes to the door with a child on her hip. The sheriff asked, "Where's Quincy?"

She answers, "He's a sleep."

"I bet he is. What time did he get home this morning?" The sheriff asked.

"I don't know. I was sleeping when he got in."

"Do any of your kids know what time he got in?"

The twenty-one-year old inside the house heard the sheriff and he knew what time his father came in, but he was not going to say anything.

She replied, "They were asleep like I was."

"Get him up. I want to talk to him."

"Okay, but he ain't going to be happy."

"Get him up!"

She went to get him while the sheriff and the deputy hold their positions. Quincy was cussing every other word as he made his way to the door. He was surprised the sheriff was already on his trail.

He leans against a post on the porch barefooted and bare-chested. "What do you want, Sheriff?"

The sheriff is wary of the behemoth of a man. "I want to know what you did with Johnny Holland last night?"

Quincy looked down and replied, "I saw him at the tavern last night and bought him a few drinks, but after that, I don't know where he went."

"I think you do, and I want you at my office right now. Get some clothes on and you're going to take a ride with us."

After a couple of hours of interrogation, the sheriff allowed him to go, but he and the deputy go get C.R. He informed C.R., the judge will go light on him if he'll admit that Quincy done away with Johnny. C.R. was as stubborn as Quincy and they stuck to their story.

The next few days, the sheriff worked tirelessly

talking to possible witnesses. He felt he may have enough to charge and hold them, but he needed to find Johnny's body.

He wasted no time in placing a search team together. They combed the woods around the area until the rain came down for two weeks. They regrouped after the rains stopped and began the search again. He had sixty volunteers, mostly from out of the county because of the Majors' influence on the people in the county. Joey was with them every step of the way.

Joey's mother was in hysteria — grieving about her cherished son. Joey couldn't say anything to her because he wasn't much better than her. He relieved his stress by searching for Johnny.

When the search began to wane, the sheriff decided the rivers and creeks needed to be dragged. He lost some volunteers, but he gained some from the fisherman that fished the area. The sheriff acquired more large hooks from other counties and the game wardens joined in the quest with their own equipment.

After a week, they had drug the bayous, creeks, and river for the body without any sign of Johnny's body. Everyone began to give up, but the exhausted sheriff and Joey. The sheriff talked the local game warden and neighboring county warden in extending the search, on the river, to the edges of the next county.

The morning was cold, and the leafless trees were engulfed in the high water from the river. The few remaining men drug for a mile into the next county. Suddenly, the hooks caught something. They thought it was a log that floated up because they had hung many of them during their search.

As the game warden and his attendant raised the

line, they saw the blond hair rise to the surface and the withered body. They thought it was Johnny but needed someone to positively identify him. They pulled him into the boat and wrapped him in a tarp. The warden yelled to the sheriff and Joey across the river.

As the sheriff and Joey approached the warden's boat, they started to raise the tarp off the body, but Joey saw one of the arms hanging out with all the scars from the dog bites.

Joey shook his head and said, "There's no need for that because I already know it's Johnny because of the scars I see on his arm."

The warden looked at the sheriff and the sheriff shook his head indicating to keep him covered. Joey knew Johnny was not coming back, but the finality of it hits him hard. He can only hold his head down with his mind attempting to accept Johnny will not be coming back ever again. The sheriff told the warden to bring him to the coroner's office and he would be there soon. He saw the pain that Joey was enduring. There was nothing for him to ease Joey's pain. Time would have to do that the sheriff thought, but he didn't know how powerful the bond was between Joey and Johnny.

When they got back to the sheriff's office, the sheriff told Joey, "You have a difficult time ahead of you. If you would rather me tell your mother, I will."

"Joey held his head down and hesitated to respond. "I'll do it. Thanks for your tireless effort, sheriff." He turned away and walked to the truck.

Joey drove on instinct toward home but had to stop and wail away. The only person that truly loved him was gone forever. He would have to face this world alone the rest of his life. Liz was the only person left that means anything to him, but does she really care for him?

Chapter Sixteen
The Day of Judgment

Joey drove up to the house and sat in the truck before going in and informing his mother of Johnny's end. He did not know anything about religion, but he had always heard that prayer helped in times of need. He prayed that he and his mother would somehow overcome the death of Johnny.

He went inside the house where his mother laid on the bed with one forearm over her forehead. Looking at her since she had suffered so much because of Johnny's disappearance, he contemplated the inevitable.

She raised her forearm and saw Joey standing in the doorway. She saw by his grim look that bad news was coming. "Mother, we found Johnny's body today. I don't know what to tell you because I feel as bad as you do." He walks away to the barn and finds a bottle Johnny stashed for when he ran out of liquor.

After a few sips, he hears a gunshot from the house. He was afraid that she would do something like that. He returned to the house and saw her laying there with blood oozing from her head. He was saddened because he never really got to know her because she never allowed him too. Johnny was her one and only, just as he was to him.

Joey drove back to town and told the sheriff what happened. The sheriff looked stunned as if there was already enough suffering for one day. He said, "Damn them Majors. I'm going to arrest Quincy and C.R. right now." He calls the deputy on the radio to come assist him in the arrest.

"Joey, I'm going to send the coroner for your mother. I'll call my wife for you go to our house right now. You don't need to be alone right now."

Joey nodded his head. The sheriff and deputy went to arrest the Majors. While Joey waited for the sheriff's wife, he contemplated to kill the Majors, but he thought perhaps justice would prevail.

When Joey arrived at the sheriff's home and his wife greeted him with a hug. She made coffee for them and read scriptures from the Bible to him. He didn't understand what she read, and he wasn't about to ask her.

The sheriff came home that evening and said, "Quincy and C.R. are in jail. Joey, I want you to stay with us tonight and if you need to stay longer, your welcome to stay on as long as you need. You have suffered two blows today that would break any man."

Joey doesn't say anything as he attempts to block any more misery from entering his mind today. At supper, he eats a small portion of his plate and excuses himself from the table. He goes to the bedroom they allowed him to stay in and cries on the bed until he cannot cry any longer.

He returned to his home the next morning and looks at the emptiness of the place. Once there was Johnny with usually a smiling face for Joey. He was someone he could talk about anything with and now his best friend and only sibling will never return.

Even his unloving mother to him—her presence will be missed. He sees the blood-stained floor where her body lay yesterday. He never understood why she disliked him. At one time, Johnny was going to tell him about his mother's affair, but he didn't because of his own state of mind and the pain it would inflict on Joey. He just never got around to telling him.

Joey sat in the barn for most of the day and finished the bottle that he started on yesterday. He went to see Liz late that afternoon. She had already heard about Joey's family. She greeted him with a hug and kiss on the cheek. "I'm so sorry, Joey. Nobody deserves what has happened to you."

Joey tried to hang on to Liz's sympathy and it helped him some. He eventually asked her to move in with him and she said, "I can't move in over there with all that death hanging about that house. I think it's cursed."

Joey continued to take care of the farm during the day and worked occasionally off the farm when he had the opportunity. He spent the evenings with Liz. But he grieved Johnny every day.

He went everyday to Johnny's gravesite and talked to him as if he was there in person. The town had donated a respectable tombstone that listed Johnny's military service. Joey thought where those people were when Johnny would sit out at the barn alone while his depression worsened.

The sheriff informed Joey that Johnny had died from drowning and he would be called as a witness at the upcoming trial for Quincy and C.R. The District Attorney had briefed Joey on his testimony and Joey ran the incidents through his mind since he could remember the first encounter with the Majors. He thought the conviction should be a given, but the more he ran the occurrences through his mind, he began to doubt if it would be enough to convict the Majors. His fears kept him up during the night.

The silence of the house and Johnny's empty bed beside him made his nights into a nightmare. He dreamed of himself on that ridge and Johnny coming to rescue him. As soon as his eyes opened, he saw Johnny's empty bed and knew it was not real.

The trial came and lasted three days. The verdict was what Joey feared—Not guilty. The Majors' lawyer made the case that Johnny was drunk and drowned himself through his own carelessness despite the river being over twenty miles away with him having no transportation to get that far. The jury said they had no evidence that the Majors drowned him.

Sheriff Gentry resigned at that time and Joey went home mad and sad. He bought a bottle of liquor and began drinking before he made it home. After a couple of hours, Joey could not accept the verdict and loaded the two shotguns and brought a hunting vest full of buck-shots. One side of the vest was loaded with twelve-gauge shells for the single shot and the other side with sixteen-gauge shells for the pump shotgun.

He gathered the guns and ammo in the front of the truck and drove to a section of woods that bordered old man Major's house. He parked the truck in the woods and put his vest on because he was going Major hunting. Off he went running through the woods with a shotgun in each hand. After a ten-minute run, he could see the Major place and as he suspected they were all there with the men sitting and standing on the porch. He counted six including Quincy's oldest boy.

Their two hog dogs started barking toward Joey. He nestled in some thick brush where he could see them, but they couldn't see him. They all looked when the dogs came running toward Joey. The dogs began baying Joey, but he ignored them as he aimed the twelve-gauge at big Quincy. One shot of buckshot dropped him from the porch. He saw a couple of them run into the house as he sprang from the bushes aiming his pump shotgun. The old man got the next load of buckshot, in the neck and head, when he went to help Quincy. At thirty yards, he stopped and shot Jock. The dogs were ripping at his legs. He butted one real hard with the stock of the gun and missed the other with it. As he turned and shot the dog, he felt a sharp pain in his chest. C.R. had thrown his large pocketknife and stuck Joey bad, but Joey went to retaliate when a gunshot grazed the top of his left shoulder. He looked and saw Willard, at the corner of the house, levering another shell into the chamber, but Joey pumped another round and blasted a round at Willard—hitting his rifle and boards at the corner of the house. Splinters ripped into his face as his gun went off barely missing Joey.

Joey looked on the porch, but there wasn't anyone there. Suddenly, C.R., from inside the front screen door, shoots a twelve-gauge double barrel shotgun at Joey with both barrels. He fail backward riddled with buckshot. C.R. and the rest of the family came out to check on the fallen family members. Jock and the old man is dead while Quincy has a pulse. C.R.'s mother told him to go get the doctor. The women folk and some of the children were crying and praying to God.

When the doctor and C.R. arrived, the doctor immediately told them that Quincy needed to be in the town clinic. As the doctor prepared the stretcher for Quincy, C.R. removed his knife from Joey's chest. Joey groaned.

C.R. said in astonishment, "Is that bastard still alive?"

The doctor heard C.R. and immediately went to the attention of Joey. "He's alive. We need to load him up with Quincy. They are in extreme danger of dying."

C.R. in a maddening voice said, "You're going to treat that bastard the same as my brother after he killed my Daddy and Jock. Look here, he'll lay here and rot before I let you treat him before my brother. Look at Willard, he needs your help. This bastard is as good as dead. You can see for yourself that he doesn't have a chance in hell."

"You're wasting time C.R." Talking to Quincy's boy, "Come on son and give us a hand in getting them loaded up."

C.R. responded, "We'll load up Quincy, but we won't load that sack of buckshot up."

The doctor said seriously. "C.R., I'll see that you are charged with murder if you insist on stalling."

C.R.'s mother said, "Go ahead and help the doctor. There's been enough misery."

They load Quincy and Joey into the truck on cushions with blankets cover them. They take them to the clinic where they are treated and given proper care.

After a week in the clinic, Quincy will survive, but Joey hangs on by a thread. The multiple wounds of bullets, knife puncture, and dog bites continue to plague his recovery. Two visitors came to visit him in the past week—Liz and the ex-sheriff. They saw him laying there with bandages wrapped around his torso and his legs. He was continually taking blood transfusions, but once he stopped losing blood, he began to gradually recover.

He was conscious of where he was and what had happened. The doctor came to check on Joey and asked, "Joey, how do you feel?"

He slowly responded, "Like a piece of meat tenderized."

"You've improved considerably since the day you were brought here. I honestly don't know how you survived, but a man with a prior machine gun bullet though his chest — it must have something to do with what the person is made of. In your case — tough as leather and a will to live."

"I don't know if that is true…I had a mission and I failed like I did on Heartbreak Ridge."

"You didn't fail. You did the best you could. Rest up. In a couple of weeks, hopefully, we'll have you walking around."

The doctor walked out, and Joey began to think about facing the law when he recovered.

Liz came to see him again and told him news that was bittersweet—she was pregnant. Joey looked at her and said, "I wished I would've known it before I shot up them Majors."

He sat up in his bed and looked at his legs and she responded, "You're worried about the law. Aren't you?"

"Yes, I am."

"Well, Joey, you should've known that I would get pregnant sooner or later."

Joey was silent. He could say a lot of things, but it would not change anything. He could only stare at his legs and wished things would have turned out different.

She began to walk out and said, "I'll come see you again, Joey."

The ex-sheriff Gentry came to see Joey and stood at the foot of the bed while Joey slept. Joey awakes from a nightmare and into one that is real.

He sees the sheriff and said, "Hello, Sheriff Gentry."

The ex-sheriff responded, "You're looking a lot better than when I came before. How soon before they release you?"

"I don't know Sheriff. They supposed to get me up out of this bed tomorrow."

"I hate to bring bad news, but I want to prepare you for what is ahead of you when they do release you." Joey stared at him and prepared for the worse. "They are going to throw the book against you. The new sheriff and the newly elected district attorney are all in with the Majors for your prosecution. You have nobody, but me to testify on your behalf. Perhaps, Liz will say some good things about you. Your counsel will look for a plea bargain and don't expect much from him. You have to give even more than you did at Quincy and C.R.'s trial. Pour your heart out to the jury. The same judge will be on the bench. I know this is not what you want to hear, but it's all you got."

Joey responded, "Sheriff, it sounds like I should've died instead of dealing with this."

"I don't blame you for what you did, but there's a consequence for everything. I may sound like a sheriff instead of your friend. You've got to be strong through this and what I know of you, you will. What about your place? Would you want to sell it to get a better lawyer?"

Joey paused and replied, "No. I have nothing else in this world. It sounds like I would be just be wasting it."

"Okay, Joey. I'm in your corner."

Chapter Seventeen
An Unbalanced System

Joey recovered to the point where he will stand trial. All the Majors fill the court room while Joey has an ex-sheriff that has little behind his name except for his tenure as sheriff and a young woman that is poor with little education.

When the Majors testify, they sob on the witness stand while Joey and his two witnesses can only tell the truth to the best of their ability.

Joey's counsel talks to him during a break. "They're seeking the death penalty. I can get you life by admitting you intended to kill the Majors."

Joey answers directly, "I intended to kill them, but I'm not admitting to it. I'll let the jury make their own decision."

He took the stand and his counsel allowed him to speak on his own behalf. The district attorney got nothing from Joey as he hammers away at him and the judge threatens him for not answering any questions.

Finally, the judge had the jury deliberate their decision. The jury gave the verdict, guilty and recommended life in prison. The judge sentenced Joey to life imprisonment without parole.

Joey was taken to Huntsville Penitentiary in Texas where he would remain the rest of his life. He was processed and checked in the prison with a weakened condition—without any health limitations. He was assigned to the Walls Unit. His cellmate is Jed Williams—a three-time felon convicted with two armed robberies and murder. Williams was a white male five-feet-eleven inches tall and one-hundred-ninety pounds, brown hair and brown eyes, and thirty-four years old. He had an uncaring attitude that Joey cannot relate with and he realized they will not be communicating that much.

The year is 1954 and the prison consisted of 50% white, 30% black, 15% Hispanic, and ninety-one women. In 1955, the deinstitutionalization of the mentally ill began by closing mental hospitals and the prisons eventually took the mentally ill into their facility.

Joey and Jed stood outside the cell while a new set of bunkbeds were squeezed into their cell. Joey and Jed received a new cellmate, Curtis Still, from one of the closed mental hospitals. He was thirty-years old and similar stature to Joey, but less stout. He was quiet and slightly disturbed.

Joey attempted a conversation with him. Unknowingly of his past, Joey asked, "Where do you come from, James?"

"I was in Rusk Hospital."

Joey had heard about Rusk from Johnny, but Jed knew of it and said, "You were in the crazy house. Right?"

"I call it a hospital. You can call it whatever you like."

Joey realized that he had mental problems and he thought of Johnny and himself. "My brother was in them kind of hospitals. It was hell to him."

Curtis asked, "Any worse than this dungeon?"

Joey replies, "I don't know. I can only go by what he told me. As far as this, I hate this damn place, but they sent me here for life. I don't think I'll ever get use to it. Nobody likes you here, but I guess nobody likes you there either?"

"There was a few that are pretentious. Joey and Jed don't understand the word 'pretentious.' Jed said with a sneer, "Do we have an educated jerk among us?"

Nothing is said.

As the sentence continued for them that year, a law was passed that slightly improved the conditions at the prison. It was still harsh and brutal. Joey worked in the fields performing agricultural work. He knew about hard work in the fields and it allowed him to get outside which he liked better than working inside the prison facilities. Sometimes, he thought he was at home working on the family farm, but he realized that wasn't reality when he looked up to see all the uniformed prisoners working in the fields. He thought about escape, but where would he go if he somehow escaped. If he went back to the farm, they would surely find him.

While Joey preferred working outside, Jed worked in the prison industries and Curtis worked in laundry.

One day, he was surprised that he had a visitor waiting for him. It was Liz and their nine-month old daughter, Rachel. He smiled for the first time since he saw her in the hospital. She returned the smile and held up their daughter for him to see her as close as she can.

They pick up the phone and Liz asked, "Isn't she pretty? She looks like you a lot. I had to bring her here for you to see her."

Joey smiles and replies, "She is gorgeous. She looks like you too with those blue eyes and her face. What is her name?"

"No, she has your brown hair, nose, and the shape of your eyes. Her name is Rachel." She smiles at Joey.

Joey nods his head and hesitates to ask, but he does. "What took you so long to come?"

She closes her eyes and said, "I didn't know what to do."

As she opened her eyes and looked at him, he responded, "Yeah. It's a bad situation."

They looked at each other without smiling, she asked with reluctance, "How are you doing?"

"It's nothing I care to talk about."

"I know." The conversation went stale and she said. "I'll try to come see you again."

"I would like that."

She said goodbye and hangs up the phone and walks away with Rachel. Joey can only fight back the tears. He slowly got up and was taken back to his cell.

His cell was one of the quieter ones in the wing. The three had little in common. Jed had been in prison twice before and he knew the ropes better than Joey and the neurotic Curtis. Joey stayed to himself and only had very brief conversations with anyone.

Usually when Joey's head hit the pillow, he went to sleep quickly, but this night he could not stop thinking about Liz and Rachel. He tossed and turned until he grew tired. Feeling himself falling asleep until he heard

Jed whispering vulgar words. He peered down from his bunk and saw Curtis's leg hanging from Jed's bunk. He was not sure what was going on until he listened more closely. What little innocence Joey had was lost that night. He knew about homosexuality but had never been around it. It bothered him even after Curtis went back to his bunk and until a couple of hours before count-up when he fell asleep. A rough day was headed for Joey.

While in the field working, Joey's mind began to think about Jed and Curtis. He wondered how long their sexual relationship had been going on. Jed must have found a weakness in Curtis that he did not find in Joey. Joey was small compared to most inmates, but he was built solid and did not show any sign of weakness. He had grown up tough with the assistance of Johnny and the Korean War and feared no one, even the unknown. Pain was second nature to him, but he still felt it every day. Most every night, he thought about the stars and Johnny. Where did they go, he wondered? They were there most every night. Now, they are gone forever. He fought back tears many times throughout the night.

His second year of imprisonment passed. He went to church services on Sundays to relieve himself of the doldrums of prison life. It is about the only time, men smiled while facing their adversity. Johnny does not think much about the scriptures or the singing, but he enjoys being amongst the happiness. Also, he enjoyed the prisoners' testimony. He was so quiet that he is rarely noticed amongst the active congregation. One Sunday, the minister asked for someone that had never testified.

He points to Joey and asked, "How about you young

man? I have seen you here every Sunday and I'm sure, you have something you could share."

Joey was silent and finally states, "I have nothing to share."

The minister responded, "I'm sure you do. We will wait until you're ready."

Joey thought about it long and hard for the next week. He realized that he could not show any weakness to his fellow inmates.

To his surprise, he received a letter from Liz stating that she intended to bring Rachel to see him at the beginning of next month. She wished him well, but she again didn't say she loved him. Although he wanted more from her, a feeling of happiness came to him because they were coming to see him.

Joey thought about a testimony for church several times during the week. When testimony time came at the church service, the minister allowed someone to give a statement. After that, the minister asked if anyone else would care to share their testimony. Joey stood up and the minister acknowledged him to come up to the mic and provide his testimony.

Joey looked down when he began to speak. "I've never been any good at speaking to a group of people...I thought about this after the minister asked me last week. I do have things that I need to say. I'm from a small farm about 100 miles from here. My older brother, Johnny, was the only thing that kept me going and he was everything to me. He was called for service in WWII and escaped death with a lot of bad wounds. He was captured by the Nazis and was sentenced to death, but because of his will to survive, he fought them and won. When he arrived home, he had survived the wounds to his body, but not his mind. He was messed up and never recovered after over 100 shock treatments in a mental ward. He was killed by a family that hated us for being poor. I took revenge and that is how I'm in here. They wrote about all his medals in the local newspaper, but no one helped him while he was alive. That's all I've got to say."

An ovation is given for Joey. The minister said, "Last week you said that you had nothing to say. God worked on you the past week brother and you delivered today."

When the church service was over, many inmates shook his hand and some even hugged him. It was the first time he had received friendliness from anyone in that prison since he had been locked up. Some even talked to him, but the guards reminded them they were in prison.

One of the guards said to them as they exited. "Now, yawl find God. Ain't that something?"

Joey was happy inside himself for the first time since Johnny was alive. He even thanked God for his happiness.

Joey expected Liz and Rachel any day, but they never came. Months went by until he lost hope that they would come. He withdrawn into a shell again and quit attending church services.

When he was in the yard lifting weights, occasionally some of the church attendees asked him when he would return. He just slightly shook his head.

It had been seven years since he arrived at the prison, he was already hard, but time had hardened him as hard as they come. He got out of the fields and was assigned to a bus-repair shop within the prison. He learned quickly and liked the change. The fields had aged him beyond his twenty-eight years of age.

Curtis was now working in a garment factory within the prison. He hoped for parole in the coming months. Jed continued working in prison industrial operations.

Unexpectedly, Liz and Rachel shows up at the visitor's area. Joey had tried to forget them, but he saw them for curiosity.

Standoffish Joey picks up the phone to the unemotional Liz and asked, "Why are you here?"

She replied, "I wanted you to see your daughter before she gets any older. She's growing into a wonderful girl."

Rachel stares at Joey. He asked, "Does she know who I am?"

"Kind of. Joey, I got married a few years back and Stan is her father now, but I want her to see her first father. This is your first father, Rachel. Say hello to Joey."

She said hello and Joey said, "I want to talk to her. Put her on the phone."

Rachel holds the phone to her ear and Joey speaks to her. "Hello, Rachel. You sure are pretty. Does everyone tell you how pretty you are?"

She shrugs her shoulders and responded, "Thank you. Why are you talking to us through that window?"

"You need to ask the warden that. Tell him that your Daddy wants to kiss and hold you."

"Are you really my Daddy?"

"I am. Your mother can explain that to you better. Tell me about school."

"How did you know I started school?"

"I keep track of things like that. I want to know what my daughter is doing."

"Well, I go to a big school. The bus picks me up in the morning and takes me home in the afternoon. There is a bunch of kids in my room. The teacher is teaching us how to print and read. We have recess and we have fun."

She stares at Joey after she speaks waiting for him to say something. He responded, "I want you to be the smartest in the class. I wasn't much good in school, but my older brother helped me."

"You have a brother. I want a baby brother or sister. Maybe, your big brother could talk to the boss and get you out from behind that window."

"I wish he could."

Liz said to Rachel, "Tell him goodbye because we'll have to leave soon.?"

Rachel said, "I'm going to have to go now. Goodbye."

Joey stops her from hanging up the phone. "Will you come see me again?"

She smiles at him and nods her head. "I'll tell mom for us to come see you. Bye."

Rachel got on the phone and said, "Joey, I don't know when we'll be back. Stan doesn't like me coming here."

Joey responded, "I can understand that, but I would like to see my daughter more. Ask him if he was in here would want to see his daughter once every five years and maybe, he'll understand."

"He doesn't think like that, Joey. I better go." They leave with Rachel staring back at him waving goodbye.

Joey was in shock after the visit. He asked himself, 'did this really occur?'

He returned to his cell disbelieving what really happened, but another surprise occurred. Curtis's bed was stripped of everything. He asked Jed, "Where's Curtis?"

Jed replied, "Something happened at his job. They've moved him to the looney tune ward."

"What happened?"

"I don't know. I haven't seen him. They just came in here and took the sheets off his bed and said he wouldn't be back. I asked them what happened and one of the guards told me that he was going to a ward where he belonged. You can take it from there."

Joey knew Curtis had mental problems, but he had been a cellmate for the last few years without getting too crazy. He did not agree with his relationship with Jed, but they did him no harm.

Chapter Eighteen
The Hit

It didn't take long before his bunk was filled by another, Jack Finley, that claimed he was serving life for a crime he did not commit. Joey did not say anything, but he saw Jed sizing up the six-foot string bean.

Jed said, "The prison is full of guys like you that claim they never did anything wrong. You see, Joey and I admit to our crimes. So, we don't want to hear any crying and bellyaching."

Joey responded, "Ease off, Jed. He might be innocent."

Jed responded, "He might, but like I said, I don't want to hear any of that whining. We got a peaceful little cell and I want to keep that way."

Joey asked, "Jack, where you from?"

Jack replied, "Palestine. I lived there all my twenty-five years."

Joey was in a talkative mood after his visit from Rachel and Liz. "What did you do in Palestine?"

"I was a carpenter until they railroaded me in here."

"I feel I got a raw deal, but here I've been for seven years and we'll be here the rest of our lives. They'll probably put you in construction with your experience as a carpenter. That'll keep your mind from thinking of your past and by the time you get in bed, you're ready to sleep."

Jack asked, "Do you ever get used to being in here?"

Joey replied, "Well, no. You just can't think about it and after some time, it gets to be a habit."

Jack just shakes his head in questioning his place in life.

The following year, they get another cellmate, Tom Bastille, that is serving forty years for murder. In fact, the whole prison population is increasing rapidly with mostly murderers. Changing and repairing bus tires had grown old. Joey started taking classes on whatever he could because his mind needed stimulation.

Things were improving for Joey, but one night, Jed and Tom were attempting to rape Jack. It woke Joey and he immediately sprang from his bunk and grabbed Jed from silencing Jack with his pillow. Joey and Jed were fighting while the wiry Jack was preventing Tom from having his way with him. Tom turned away from him and helped Jed attack Joey. He was holding his own against Jed, but with two bigger men, it turned into a wrestling match with the two of them throwing haymakers too. Joey was hoping Jack would come help because he was absorbing a lot of heavy blows and couldn't hold out much longer. Finally, Jack grabbed Tom from behind and began to pull him off Joey, but the two-hundred-pound Tom slammed his elbow into the thin man's gut which backed him off and Tom pummeled him to the floor.

The other cells of prisoners could hear the fighting and it sounded life-threatening. One cell of prisoners started dragging their cups across the bars to get the attention of the guards. By the time the guards arrived, Jed had beaten, kicked, and stomped Joey. He was beaten bad and Jack was knocked unconscious. Immediately, the guards shackled the two ruffians and took them away while one of the guards radioed for medical assistance.

Jack regained consciousness and was released back to his bunk. Joey had a fracture in his neck, broken nose, and a cut mouth. He was admitted into the prison hospital. While in recovery, he and the three other cellmates were interrogated individually. It did not take long for the panel to figure out what transpired despite Jed and Tom saying they were attacked by Joey and Jack but with different stories. Jed and Tom received sixty days in the hole while Joey received fifteen days after he was released from the hospital. Jack was cleared but given six-months' probation. No one would escape completely after such a disturbance whether they were innocent or not.

As Joey sat out his time in the hole, he realized he was in a place where he would never be given any type of break. Since he had a lot of time to think about everything, he wondered about Rachel. Perhaps, one day, she would come get him out of prison. He thought about Johnny saying he would always be there for him. He began to break down realizing his life was a waste. His service in the war got him a few medals, but they never did him any good. They sat in a drawer back on the home place if somebody had not already taken it from him. Neither Johnny nor Rachel would be coming to rescue him. He was doomed forever.

When Joey returned to his bunk, two other prisoners

had been assigned to the cell. One was a murderer, Timothy Garcia, and the other, Bobby Mason, was in for armed robbery. He smiled at Jack and introduced himself to Timothy and Bobby. They seemed friendly enough. Jack smiled as they conversed.

As the months passed, Joey returned to the yard to lift weights. The other prisoners went their own way in the yard. Joey always kept his shirt on when lifting to avoid anyone making something of his scars he received during the Major shootout. He did not lose much strength while he was away. He saw Tom staring at him while he was bench pressing. Once he finished his reps, he looked to find Tom still staring at him.

He turned away, but Tom said, "Why don't you take your shirt off so everyone can see all the scars that got you into this nightmare?"

The prisoners standing by, looked at Joey, but Joey only looked down to the ground. Joey glanced at Tom and he was still staring at him. It seemed that Tom had it in for him. The sixty days in solitary confinement only made Tom more malicious. As they exited the yard, a commotion ensued. Joey kept his distance from the trouble and walked inside the walls as he saw Jed giving him an intent look.

When the cell doors closed, Jack was not there. "Joey asked Timothy and Bobby, "Did either one of you see Jack?"

They both shook their heads. Joey knew at least one of them saw Jack, but they weren't going to let themselves get involved.

Finally, they came to clean out Jack's bunk. Joey knew he would probably be next without any idea when it was coming. It could be this week or six months, but it was coming.

Joey continued his normal schedule with caution. In the yard, Tom's presence was always looming near and Jed was seen occasionally. Joey knew it would probably be a hired assassin and that could be anybody. He knew not to report anything to the guards or someone in authority because the general population was already keeping an eye on him since he could be a snitch after Tom and Jed's two-month hole punishment. A snitch was regarded worse than any defilement.

As the months passed, Joey knew that his guard had most likely let down some, but he knew this was the time for a hit. Renewed caution would have to be of utmost importance for his survival. He remembered when he was ascending that ridge and how cautious he had to be from getting his head blown off. He did not worry about his head getting his head blown off, but he worried about his vitals being gouged by a shank. What if two assassins come for him. He contemplates how he would defense such a hit. He began to think that he will have to take his chances regardless the type of assault.

While he bench pressed in the yard, an assassin sunk his shank into Joey's chest. Joey threw the barbells from over the top of him and fell off the bench. The prisoners that was bench pressing went to cover him and attempt to assist him. The guards blew the whistle for the prisoners to go to the ground.

As they cleared the prisoners from the yard, guards surrounded the seriously wounded Joey and called for the medics to his attention. He nearly bled to death, but the young war horse would survive another near-death experience. He would be kept under protective custody. Two near-deaths for one prisoner within a year was something the prison was attempting to avoid. No one would provide any information on the assassin.

Joey fully recovered from the deadly wound. He was placed in a special housing unit where he was away from the Walls unit and rarely in contact with other prisoners. He would have liked it if it was not for the isolation and idleness.

The new Director of Texas Prisons, George Beto, had been employed as college administrator and ordained minister who had served six years on the corrections board. He expanded religious counseling and basic education under his watch. Although profit and punishment remained the Texas prison motto, Beto did improve the prison system for the better. He did not approve of any prisoners being idle. Ten hours of work a day was required and everything should be cleaned and polished. Even the fields had to be manicured to his approval. He expected nothing less of his staff.

Convicts complained he came to Texas with a bible in one hand and a bat in the other. Texas remained the lowest cost per prisoner in the entire nation. Texas prisons were peaceful with the use of force and fear.

Joey took advantage of all that Beto enacted that would benefit him. As the years went by, he was transferred to the Ellis Unit named after the director Beto replaced when Oscar Ellis died while in office. Aware that Jed and Tom remained in the Walls Unit, he wondered if they would send another assassin after several years had passed since the last attempt on his life. He had improved his education and now worked in construction. He had quit working out in the yard because of being an easy target in a defenseless position. Running replaced his yard time as a few others also ran. He remained in good condition by working out in his cell—realizing that his physical condition had assisted him in his recovery of the many wounds he had survived throughout his lifetime.

A new cellmate named Bill Jennings was to become a friend of his. They were the same age and were slow in getting to know each other. He saw Joey without his shirt on and said in a startling voice, "My god, how are you still alive with all that damage to your body?"

Joey replied, "I guess it wasn't my time."

"Did you get that before you came in here?"

"All but the puncture wound on my chest."

"You've had a helluva a life."

"Yeah. Korean War got me the big bullet wound that went straight through me and the others ended me up in here."

"You are one tough sonofabitch. I never seen anything like it."

"My life has been a tough one since I was born. How about you?"

Bill replies, "It evidently wasn't as rough as yours, but I hadn't caught many breaks except the ones that broke my ass."

Joey responded, "I've been in here for nearly twenty years and the prison population has grown to the point where convicts are having to sleep on the floor."

"They'll have to add on to these units or build new prisons. You said you've been here for nearly twenty years—where were you before they moved you in here?"

"The Walls Unit."

"That's where I was for five years when I was in prison before."

"Did you make the same mistake twice?"

"Sort of, but this time a partner caused me to get locked up. He didn't do as I told him and when we got caught, they talked him into testifying against me since I was a repeat offender. He got off on probation and I got twenty years."

"You won't have to serve all of that. I've seen convicts serve less than half their sentences. By the way, don't get used to just the two of us being in here. They're sending two more in here tomorrow."

William responded, "I was wondering why prisoners are sleeping on the floor while you're in here alone."

"I've been in protective custody the last few years. They slipped me in over here a few months ago. I guess my time of being alone is over again."

"Joey, do you prefer being alone?"

He replied, "Sometimes, but a good conversation like we're having helps me to enjoy being around people."

William reached out his hand and said, "Joey, I'm your friend and don't forget that."

Joey shook his hand and said, "I appreciate that."

The next day, the two new prisoners showed up one at a time. The first one was slightly taller than Joey and weighed about the same. The twenty-three-year old brown-haired and blue-eyed prisoner was Adrian Dubose — serving ten years for armed robbery.

The second was a thirty-year old, Brody Miles, that was nearly six-foot tall and one-hundred-eighty pounds. He had dirty-blond hair and blue eyes. He was serving twenty-years for robbery and attempted murder. Also, he had a cocky attitude that he revealed on his initial meeting with his cellmates.

Chapter Nineteen
As Time Passes By

Adrian treats Joey and Bill with respect since they are convicts that are considerably older. Brody thought everybody was dumb compared to him. He particularly picked on Adrian, but he was sharp with the tongue on anyone that did not agree with him.

While Brody was working in the garment factory, Bill told Adrian. "If Brody starts being physically with you, don't put up with it. Joey and I will stop it if he gets too rough with you. You got to show him that you're no easy prey."

Adrian responded, "I'm not used to this. They had me over at the Wynne Unit and they kept everyone so beat down that most of the cons never said a cross word to anyone."

"At least you have some prison experience. Brody hasn't seen the brutal world of prisons, yet. He thinks he's bad, but he's just a bug in a den of red ants."

Everyone in the cell attempted to avoid any communication with Brody. Finally, one night before bedtime, he got mad because no one would talk to him. "What's with you assholes? None of you says a word to me."

No one says a word which infuriates Brody even

more. He kicks both bottom bunks and yells, "Fuck you motherfuckers!"

Joey and Bill look at one another since they are sitting on those bunks, but still no one says a word. He grabs Adrian's mattress and yanks it while he is laying on it. Adrian struggles to not fall from the bunk. The close quarters in the cell has everyone in harm's way. Finally, Joey and Bill look at each other and decide that Brody needs to be taken down a notch or two. Joey wraps his arms around Brody's legs and picks him up and pushes him against the wall. Brody unleashes a tirade of punches on Joey's head. Bill grabs Brody around the head and pulls him down to the floor which enables them to hold Brody down and calm him down.

Bill said to him, "Ease up Brody or we can get rough on you. Do you understand?"

"Get off of me or I'll kick each one of your asses."

Bill said, "We're not letting you up until you calm down and really mean it."

Brody continued to struggle under the weight of Bill and Joey. Bill placed a choke hold on Brody and tightened his grip until Brody started losing consciousness. Then he relaxed the choke hold seeing that Brody was no longer a threat. Joey and Bill sat on their bunks closely watching Brody gasping for air.

Adrian placed his mattress back on his bunk and said, "That ought to teach that sorry ass a lesson."

Joey responded, "Let's hope it did. I don't want anymore trouble with him or anybody else."

Brody was quiet as the months passed and the cell was peaceful. Conversations occurred and only occasionally, he would let out a condescending response while the others did not acknowledge his spewing poison. They would tolerate him unless he became violent again.

The year is 1972 and there is a changing of the guard from the TDC Director George Beto who resigned when he had to pay Attorney Frances Jalet and her prison clients $10,000 for court costs after he had maliciously discredited and terminated her for attempting to expose his slavery tactics that he planned to keep under wraps at all costs from the press and public. A year later, he died.

The United States began an incredible expansion of prisons at the federal and state level. The number of prisoners increased from less than two million to seven million. Forty-four percent of the prison population in Texas was African Americans, thirty-nine percent was Anglo- Americans, and seventeen percent Mexican-Americans. Females was less than four percent.
W.J. Estelle had become the TDC Director after Beto resigned. Estelle was a warden in Montana when he met Beto. They became friends and Beto wanted him as his successor. Estelle liked Beto's prison system model and intended to keep it humming along. It was hard to believe that he was even less compromising than Beto when it came to battle the prisoners and their representatives in and out of court. His troubles was just beginning.

It was mid-1974, Joey, Adrian, and Bill became good friends while Brody made some attempts to fit in, but he just lacked the courtesy that was required to gain the trust of his cellmates.

Meanwhile, in the Walls Unit at the Education/Library Building, three Mexican inmates

took control of the building and took eleven prison workers and four prisoners hostage. Arms

had been smuggled into the prison for the three inmates. The leader, Fred Carrasco, a heroin

kingpin in South Texas, was serving a life sentence for the attempted murder of a police officer.

He was also suspected in the murder of dozens of people in Mexico and Texas. The FBI and the

Texas Rangers assisted the Walls Unit. The convicts made some demands and they were met

with tailored suits, dress shoes, toothpaste, cologne, walkie-talkies, and bullet proof helmets.

Carrasco said they were fleeing to Cuba. After eleven days, the convicts made their dangerous

attempt to escape. Making a makeshift shield around their vehicle with eight hostages and inside

the vehicle were three convicts and four hostages while the prison guards and Texas Rangers

were prepared with fire hoses. They blasted the vehicle with the hoses, but a rupture in the hose

provided the convicts time to kill the two women hostages who had volunteered to join the

convicts in the armored car. The prison personnel returned fire, Carrasco committed suicide and

one of the convicts was killed. The surviving convict received death row at Joey's unit, Ellis, and

was executed.

Joey and the other inmates in Ellis Unit had received enough information concerning the siege that they knew tougher measures would be taken against the whole prison population.

In October 1976, Joey, Adrian, Bill, and Brody go to the convict rodeo with their one-
time ticket for the year. None were participants because none had never been to a rodeo in their
pre-prison years. Joey and Bill had been on a horse before, but never had the opportunity to
experience any rodeo skills. There were some participating that had less experience than that.
They enjoyed getting out of the prison facility and they found the show extremely entertaining.
They picked their favorite cowboys and cheered them on throughout the contests. Another
favorite for them was the Hard Money Event. Forty Inmates with red shirts were turned into the
arena with a raging wild bull with a Bull Durham tobacco sack tied between its horns. The object
was for some brave inmate to get the sack and take it to the Judge. Fifty dollars had been placed
in the sack, but donations often ran the pay up, sometimes to fifteen-hundred dollars. It was action-packed and exciting for everyone. That made Joey and Brody want to participate in the upcoming year event.
Once back in the cell, the fun soon returned to the doldrums of prison life. Brody had finally adapted to his cellmates and became a participant in the evening conversations.

Joey formed more friendships as his long stay in prison continued. One was a black inmate named Truman. Truman had been a Black Panther member in the seventies and carried a chip on his shoulder. He was serving a life sentence for murdering a white man. Joey and he got off to a bad start in the yard. He taunted Joey as a little cracker which Joey knew the word too well from his family being harassed by the Majors.

Gangs became more relevant in the 1980s and the Aryan brotherhood saw Truman as a threat to not only to a thirty-year lifer, but also to the entire white inmates. They came forward to Joey if he needed their protection, but he refused. He wanted no part of the gang and he was getting of an age that he did not care whether he was killed or not.

He told Truman that he meant him no harm, but others would if he continued his bad-mannered behavior. Truman was angry, but he started respecting Joey. From then on, they acknowledged each other's presence with respect.

In 2015, a group of young attorneys reopened Joey's case and proceeded to expose that he was not given a fair trial. Joey was eighty-one years old and had served more than enough time for a fair review of his trial.

They had talked to Joey and were convinced that he was railroaded by the judge, jury, and the Majors' influence.

Chapter Twenty
A Distant Society

After a tremendous effort by his defense lawyers, Joey will soon be released. He cannot believe he will soon be free from the life he had grown accustomed to after sixty-five years. He contemplated what he would do when he was finally out of the prison system. He wants to go home, but he knows there will be nothing there.

A new cellmate was imprisoned for possession of drugs and selling them. Hector begun to enlighten Joey on the world outside.

"Man Joey, I can't even explain how much things have changed since you've been in here. I wasn't even born until 1984."

Joey said, "I've heard a lot over the years."

Hector said, "Man, the law is everywhere. The pull you over for barely going over the speed limit. You don't even have to go over the speed limit and they'll pull you over. They are looking for anything to score big — DWI, possession, anything on your record."

"Well, I probably won't be driving."

"The world has changed big time. Everyone uses cell phones for everything."

"I heard about that."

"Are you going to buy one?"

Joey shakes his head and replied, "I doubt it. I have no one to call and no one is going to call me."

"Well… you know, there a must. You know everyone has to have one."

"I'll try my best to not have one. I won't have the money for things like that."

"What are you going to do without a car and cellphone?"

"I'll probably spend some time at the library and watch TV."

"Don't let them put you in one of those old people home. They won't let you go anywhere."

"No. I won't be going to one of those. They've been talking to me about getting me in one. I told them no and I'm going to enjoy being free. That sounds like another kind of prison."

Hector shook his head with aggravation and said, "It won't be free like you were when you came in here. You have to pay for every damn thing and watch out for the new shysters. They'll tell you something is free, and you'll be getting money taken out of your bank account without knowing it. You got a lot of unknowns to face out there."

Joey shrugged his shoulders and said, "I know I do. I'll just face the problems one at a time."

"Good luck with that. I can hook you up with some drug pushers."

"No thanks."

Hector said convincingly, "Easy money and they'll take care of you when you tell them I sent you."

"No. I've been kind of orphan all my life. I'll just have to deal with it as it comes."

Hector pointed his finger at Joey and said, "One

last thing. People are as fucked up as people in here. Just remember that."

The word is out in the prison that old Joey would no longer be a fixture at the prison after sixty-five-years. The prisoners could not believe the old timer would no longer be there. He had become as much of a feature as the walls of the prison — the longest serving prisoner in prison at the time.

He had seen thousands of prisoners pass through the gates and many of those returned. He knew many of the convicts that were executed during his stay. The new generations of prisoners that he observed were each different and less respective as time went forward. He knew the world on the outside would be callous and unforgiving of his past.

The day came that Joey had been hoping for sixty-five-years. He was gathering his belongings as fellow prisoners watched from their cells. Bill was sad that he was losing his long-term cellmate and friend.

Tears came to Bill's eyes as he spoke, "You be careful out there. The world is like night and day since you came here back in the fifties. I wish I could be with you, but it looks like I'm going to die in here."

Joey contemplated the circumstances and responded, "We never know what lies in front of us. I appreciate your concern and I hope you get out of here soon. I've enjoyed your friendship and would like to have you on the outside. I have to go just to see how it feels and I've got a daughter out there I would like to find."

The guards came to escort him to the discharge

department. He was waiting and ready to go when they arrived. He hugged Bill and the old timer walked with the guards toward the exit. Truman saw Joey leaving and he began to sob watching a friend he knew had served a very long sentence that was probably uncalled for. He wished that he would have got to known Joey more. As he walked through the prison, inmates saw that he was truly being released. They began to clap and gave him a standing ovation.

He walked straight ahead with the guards and never responded to any of the fanfare. Once they came to a stairway, the guards asked if he needed assistance in crossing, but he declined any help.

Once they reached the discharge office, he was given a change of clothes and the clothes he wore in 1954. They asked if he had someone to pick him up.

"I have no one." He thought about possibly his daughter, but he had not heard from her since the fifties. He watched one guard fooling around with his cellphone and another talking to his wife on the phone about going to see a rock band. The clock on the wall caught his attention as he watched the minutes pass by. 'This is finally it,' he thought to himself about being out from behind the prison walls."

The checkout prison official shakes his head as he stamps the documents for his freedom. "I wish you luck Joey. You're going to need it after sixty-five-years being away from it. It'll be like landing on another planet."

The official unlocked the door with a switch and a guard opens it for him to depart. The guard walks him from outside the building to a gate for him to exit the prison walls.

Once on the edge of the street in front of the prison, Joey gazes down the road for automobiles and sees guards on horses walking toward him. They ride on by him after tilting their hats for acknowledgement. Somethings never change as he watches the prison guards on horses as he did in the 1950s. He stands there knowing his daughter will never come.

After standing by the road for half an hour, the guard on the wall yells down, "There is a bus you can catch if you go left to the stop sign. You'll see the bus stop."

Joey stood there for a few seconds and then began to walk to the left on the sidewalk. While he walks, he feels a little more freedom at each step he takes. He saw the vehicles at the parking lot, and they look like a small version of the cars that he saw during his time before prison, but most of the trucks were considerably larger than he had seen before.

Once he neared the stop sign, he saw a glass building that was partially covered and there was a bench inside. He sat there and waited. A low riding car was approaching, and he stared at the unusual bouncing of the car where sparks would occur as it hit the pavement. The passenger gave a slight wave to Joey, but he was so shocked with the vehicle that he thought something was wrong with the car.

When Joey did not wave back, the passenger shot him the finger. Joey knew what that meant, but he ignored it because he did not want trouble.

He sat there wondering what would come next. He saw a bus coming down the road and it stopped in front of him. Its doors opened and no one came out.

The bus driver asked him from his seat. Where are you going?"

Joey replied, "Where are you going?"

The bus driver used his index finger to signal for him to come nearer. "I've got a feeling you don't know for sure where you want to go. I'll drop you off wherever you like. If you need a place to stay, I can drop you off at some of the places you can afford. How about it?"

Joey stepped up into the bus and said, "I'm not sure where to go."

Joey looks back into the bus and sees the occupants seated. He notices most of them are African American. Some of the women have red and some have blonde hair which he had never seen before on a black person. He sees Whites with green hair and tattoos covering their face and what other body parts he could see. Most of the young people have rings in their noses, mouth and ears. He even sees a young man that had pointed ears and sharp teeth.

He sat down in a seat near the front and clearly understood that he was on a different planet. Joey would no longer be on the prison roll call that he had been on since 1954 to 2019. He wondered what Johnny would have said about this new world.

The End